THE
MURDERER'S
SMILE

Kevin D'Onofrio

Kevin D'Onofrio

outskirtspress

DENVER, COLORADO

Outskirts Press, Inc.
http://www.outskirtspress.com

Paperback ISBN: 978-1-4787-5225-7
Hardback ISBN: 978-1-4787-5297-4

Outskirts Press and the "OP" logo are trademarks belonging to Outskirts Press, Inc.

PRINTED IN THE UNITED STATES OF AMERICA

Many thanks are owed but this book would not be possible without the support of: Erin Baldwin, MD, Cara, Eric, Gunnther, Randy, Sheila, Susan, Tiffany and the Wombat.
Much love to all of you.

Years ago however, I made a promise that I would dedicate my first published novel to Darla Deanne Miller.
A promise is a promise. Sorry it took so long Darla.

The Murderer's Smile

As the defense rested and the judge adjourned court for the day, Tony Michaels looked lost and scared. He had once been "The Most Trusted Man in Texas," at least according to billboards all around Dallas. The former top-rated Channel 9 news anchor now stood accused of murdering his pregnant wife and young son.

The media had turned on its own with Michaels, covering him as feverishly as they covered OJ Simpson, Scott Peterson, John and Patsy Ramsey, and every national murder case since. Some thought Michaels received less of a fair shake than others with the biased coverage. Channel 9 had even aired his arrest live and trumpeted their "exclusive" footage. Since then, Michaels had become known as "The Anchor of Death" in all media coverage.

As the jury exited the room, Michaels was aware the Court of Public Opinion had long since convicted him. Despite his emotion-filled pleas, his unwavering insistence that he was innocent, and despite his legal team's best efforts, Michaels was now certain that the jury would soon return with the same verdict that his once-adoring public had already delivered.

Michaels hadn't always been a great husband and his infidelity, made public during the trial, only furthered the case against him. But he truly cared for his wife and would have never hurt her physically. He knew there was no way he could have committed this heinous crime. Unfortunately, he had no alibi, had been drinking the night of the murders. He had no recollection of the events of that night, and the evidence was stacked against him. He was now resigned to the fact that the jury would find him guilty and was trying to decide which of his two likely fates—life in prison or the death penalty—would be worse.

Michaels was fighting back tears as the courtroom emptied. A man he had never met but instantly recognized approached him and extended his hand.

"Mr. Michaels, can I get a moment of your time?" the man asked.

"Sure, but I don't know what you want from me," Michaels answered shaking the man's hand.

"Mr. Michaels, I'm William—"

"I know who you are, Mr. Gunderson. I don't mean to be rude, but I would like to get out of here. Can you get to the point?"

"Certainly, Mr. Michaels." As Gunderson spoke, Michaels noticed his well-manicured fingernails, the mirrorlike shine on his expensive shoes, and the impeccable tailoring of his custom Italian suit. There wasn't a hair out of place. Michaels immediately thought that Gunderson was born to be a politician.

"I don't mean any insult here, Mr. Michaels, and I certainly respect your feelings in this difficult time, but I believe you know what verdict the jury will have when they return," Gunderson continued. "I believe your legal team fought hard for you, but not hard enough. I would like to personally handle your appeal."

Gunderson extended his hand once again, this time offering his business card.

"Why on earth would you want to take my case?" Michaels asked, not taking the card.

"Because I believe we would win," Gunderson boasted. "I've never lost a case. With my team on the case and with me personally representing you, I am very confident that you will be acquitted and we can rebuild your reputation. I can't promise anything about your career, but you will definitely be a free man to find a place that will forgive and forget."

"I appreciate the offer, sir, but I'm not sure I can afford you, and I'm not very confident we could win the appeal."

"Well, Mr. Michaels, I am *very* confident," Gunderson said extending his card once more. "Please just take my card. Money is not a concern for me. I'll even consider taking the case pro bono, only fees to cover expenses for my team. Think about it while the jury deliberates."

Michaels took the card somewhat reluctantly as Gunderson smiled the smile of a politician, nodded his head at Michaels, and said in a very proper manner, "I shall await your call. Good day."

Michaels's attorney approached as Gunderson did a precise about-face and marched toward the exit.

"What was that all about?" the attorney asked.

"Nothing," Michaels replied, stealthily slipping the card into his pocket. "Let's get out of here."

Most people in America would recognize William H. Gunderson III from seeing him on the television—either through winning several high-profile cases or for his occasional role as a legal expert for CNN, Fox News, and more. Some knew him as a man the Republican Party was hoping to groom for a new career in politics, first governor of Texas and then eventually president.

A Wikipedia search of William H. Gunderson III could tell anybody the basics. He was high school valedictorian. Then as a cadet at West Point, Gunderson graduated top of his class and was the best marksman on campus. He served his active duty as a sniper, receiving his share of medals along the way.

When Gunderson had fulfilled his military obligations and received his honorable discharge, he used his West Point connections to get into Harvard Law. Again, he graduated top of his class and used that and some connections to land a job in the Baltimore District Attorney's office. Gunderson was undefeated as a prosecutor. He was being courted for politics, but he left public service and to the surprise of many, Gunderson became a defense attorney.

Gunderson found being a defense attorney more challenging and more exciting than being a prosecutor. He opened his own law firm in Dallas. His biggest case involved an oil billionaire accused of murdering his wife. All the evidence pointed to the oilman as the murderer, but Gunderson proclaimed his innocence all along and managed to poke enough holes in the evidence to get his man acquitted.

That case put Gunderson in the national spotlight. He would go on to take on a few high-profile cases around the country through the years and win them all.

Now, Gunderson rarely appeared in court. His law firm still bore his name, but he had essentially retired. At this point he mostly played golf, attended church regularly, did charity work and appeared on the news to provide expert analysis on the current "Trial of the Century."

That much, most people knew.

Tony Michaels would soon find out the full story on William H. Gunderson III. For the second time, his world would be flipped upside down.

The next day, closing arguments were given by both sides. The jury was given its instructions and left to begin deliberations. Michaels shook his lawyer's hand, made an attempt at a smile toward his girlfriend and left.

Back in his hotel that night, Michaels ordered room service, which made him think about what he would request for his final meal if he were to be sentenced to die. He imagined it would most likely be something from Bob's Steak and Chop House, but that was a decision for another night, if at all.

His decision tonight was easy. He had not touched alcohol since the night of the murders. Now knowing that every night until the jury returned a verdict was quite possibly his last night as a free man, it seemed like a good idea to get drunk.

The night before, Michaels asked the concierge to find him a fine bottle of scotch. He gave him some money, with an extra C-note for his trouble.

When Michaels returned to his room he found a bottle of Macallan Fine Oak twenty-one-year-old scotch waiting for him. The concierge had made a fine choice. Smiling had become a rare event for Michaels, but looking at the bottle of Macallan brought a smile to his face. It wasn't the beaming smile with his perfect white teeth that had graced so many billboards, nor was it the friendly welcoming smile as he introduced himself every night on the Channel 9 news.

No, this was not the smile viewers had grown used to. He was sure that smile was completely gone from his repertoire now. This was casual, lips together, curled slightly upward.

That, in itself, seemed like a small victory. Once a happy, successful man, the pleasures in life came very rarely for him now. But he was going to enjoy this scotch and bask in its bouquet and sweet finish.

He got up to grab his fifth or sixth glass. Michaels couldn't decide which as his tolerance was nowhere near what it used to be. Maybe it was more than six, he thought. The room didn't seem as stable as it did earlier.

As he poured the scotch, he glanced over and spotted his wallet, his room key and a business card. He vaguely remembered emptying his pockets the day before and throwing the contents toward the television on his way as he changed out of his suit.

Michaels picked up the business card and looked at it. It was a very simple business card. It was on expensive stock but simply read "W. H. Gunderson" and a phone number, which he couldn't make out through his now scotch-blurred eyes. He supposed somebody with Gunderson's reputation didn't need anything fancier, but he also expected somebody of Gunderson's reputation to have a much more boastful business card.

Michaels took his last drink of scotch and set the glass down. Now he was really starting to feel the alcohol. The room was beginning to spin, and he needed to lie down. He went to drop the card on the table but missed, and it floated to the ground.

It landed facedown. Something was handwritten on the back. Michaels carefully bent down to pick up the card. Fortunately, the writing was large enough for his eyes to focus.

"I KNOW YOU ARE INNOCENT"

Michaels dropped the card once again. "What the fuck?" he muttered as he collapsed onto his bed and passed out.

Tony Michaels woke up the next morning at 11:17 when housekeeping knocked on his door. He fought through his hangover, got dressed and checked his phone. No messages. That was a good thing. He wasn't due in court any time soon. He threw on his Dallas Cowboys hat and went downstairs to get a bite to eat and let housekeeping clean his room.

As he gathered his things he noticed that there was a little less than half the bottle of Macallan. He thought he might finish it off after dinner.

Tony had been living in the hotel for months now and rarely ventured out of his room except to go to court. He would occasionally dine in the hotel restaurant. He always treated the employees well so even though breakfast was over, they had no problem when he ordered a spinach and cheese omelet with a side of hash browns and an English muffin.

As he waited for his breakfast, he popped a couple ibuprofen tablets and sipped on his coffee, hoping the headache would go away soon. He felt safe in the hotel. Miss Cook had registered him under a pseudonym and the hotel had protected his privacy well. He supposed he deserved that for paying $500 per night.

Tony ate slowly, trying to savor every bite. He wondered if it was better for him if the jury came back with a verdict quickly or took its time. He allowed himself the momentary hope of being found not guilty and thought, *What then?* Certainly his career was over. He couldn't imagine any station would hire him, and if they would, after the way he had been treated, could he work in the media again? He didn't think so. He wondered if after paying for the hotel and legal fees he would have enough money left to not have to work again. He thought he might but if not he wondered what he would do for work.

Tony wondered if he would have to leave Dallas. Leave Texas? If so, where would he go? He finally forced himself to stop asking such questions. The reporter in him wanted to know all of the answers, but pragmatically, he knew he didn't have any. He was also aware that he may never have a need to find out the answers. He had been portrayed by the prosecution as a cold, violent narcissist who drank too much, cheated on his wife and resented her for holding him back in his career.

Tony knew he was innocent, but he was honest enough to admit to himself that if he was a juror he would vote guilty based on the case presented by both sides. He finished up his breakfast and headed back to his room, figuring housekeeping should be done with his room by now.

Back in his room, Tony poured himself half a glass of scotch "Hair of the Dog," he said. Then decided to take a long, hot shower. While in the shower he realized that he was already a prisoner. Sure, he was in a very posh, comfortable, friendly prison, but it had become a personal private cell. He had been forced to sell his house to avoid the news vans parked outside. And once inside the refuge of this palatial hotel, he had been afraid to venture out.

It wasn't that long ago that Tony Michaels was welcomed anywhere in Dallas. He received more than his share of comps as well from businesses who loved celebrities visiting their establishment. He had always kept several signed 8x10s in his car in case a restaurant manager, bartender or sometimes even a customer would ask for one.

Now, he knew he wasn't welcome anywhere in town. The last time he had ventured out, he could feel the stares, see people pointing and hear the whispers. All of those 8x10s had been taken off the walls. Nobody wanted to be associated with a man accused of murdering his pregnant wife and young son.

He missed his career. He missed the adoration. He missed his favorite restaurants and hangouts. He missed his house. He missed freedom. But mostly, Tony Michaels missed his wife.

After showering, Tony took a nap hoping to sleep off the rest of his hangover. He woke when his lawyer called to let him know the jury would not be delivering the verdict today. So he had at least one more night in this luxury prison.

He was already hungry again and ordered a bacon cheeseburger from room service. He also ordered a bucket of ice and twelve bottles of Stella Artois. He would have preferred Innis & Gunn, but that was hard to find in Dallas so he settled for the Stellas. He decided the rest of the Macallan would wait until the verdict was read.

The burger was excellent, and the Stella was more than adequate. He turned on the television and found it ironic that *The Shawshank Redemption* was on. Andy Dufresne was certainly a kindred spirit to Michaels, but Tony knew his prison experience would be vastly different than Andy's and there would be no chance of tunneling his way out with a rock hammer. He decided that in the unlikely event he was acquitted, he would take a trip to Zihuatanejo.

Michaels took a cold sip of beer, wishing he were in Zihuatanejo. He closed his eyes and tried to imagine the feel of the sand under his feet and the smell of the ocean. When his mind returned to his beautiful hotel room prison, he finished off his beer and wondered aloud how he got here in the first place.

Anthony Vincenzo Michaels grew up in a blue-collar suburb of Chicago. His earliest memories were of sitting in his father's lap watching the evening news. Young Tony loved watching the news. He was fascinated by the anchors in their fancy suits with their perfect hair. The anchors didn't look like anyone he had ever seen.

His father worked in a factory and came home dirty, sweaty and exhausted most nights. The same was true of most of his neighbors. Young Tony knew he didn't want to be like that. He wanted to wear fancy suits. He wanted to be a news anchor.

Every night, young Tony would study the anchors, their mannerisms, their diction, their cadence. In his room he would practice his version of the nightly news. As he got older, when his mother would ask how his day at school went, Tony would respond in his best anchor voice, making sure to get in all the pertinent facts and would finish with "Now back to you, Mom."

As it turned out, Tony was also a gifted athlete. He didn't have much passion for sports, but they came easily and he saw it as his best chance to get into college. Tony had only played soccer and baseball growing up, but his friends convinced him to try out for football in high school.

By his freshman year, Tony Michaels was already 6-foot-1 with a lean, athletic frame. He was well-conditioned and had a strong leg from soccer. He was certain he could at least be the kicker since he didn't know how to play any positions. He was faster than his friends so they convinced Tony to also try out for wide receiver.

As the team began its first practices, the coaches liked the idea of a tall, fast receiver and also thought it would be the easiest position for him to adapt to the sport. He had by far the strongest leg on the team and was handed the jobs of punter and place kicker.

In his first game, on his first punt attempt he found his ticket to college. The play started as a disaster. The snap was awful. It was well over his head and several feet to his right. He chased after the ball, scooped it up, dodged two defenders and fired a rocket downfield to one of his teammates for a first down. After the game, the coach told him to be sure to study his playbook over the weekend because he was going to be the starting quarterback on Monday.

By his senior year, Michaels was one of the top quarterback prospects in the country, heavily recruited by all the big-time programs. Now 6-foot-4, he worked tirelessly in the weight room and worked just as hard practicing to be a quarterback as he still practiced to be a news anchor.

After leading his team to the state title and being named Illinois Player of the Year, the college football world anxiously awaited his decision. While the rest of the country had been trying to lure Michaels to their universities, Northwestern hadn't even recruited the star quarterback in their own backyard, figuring he had his choice of colleges and would opt for one of the more prestigious programs over Northwestern which has never been described as a football powerhouse.

Michaels wanted to go to Northwestern for their outstanding Broadcast Journalism department, so he wrote a letter to the Wildcats head coach, explaining his desire to attend the university. He asked if there might be a spot for him on the team, questioning why a local school didn't seem interested in him.

Coach Mercer was just as stunned reading the letter as everyone else would be when the announcement was later made. But he knew he had to act quickly before Michaels opted for a program like Notre Dame which had been doing its best to lure Michaels to play in front of Touchdown Jesus.

One day after mailing the letter to Northwestern, Michaels spent much of the school day wondering if he would hear back from the Wildcats. While he was waiting for the bus, Michaels decided he should probably go home and start researching other schools with quality Broadcast Journalism departments. Football was fun, but it wasn't the be-all and end-all for Michaels like it was for some recruits. For him, it was a means to an end. He had never wavered from his early dreams to anchor the news.

He was making a list of the schools he would investigate that night when two vans pulled up. The Northwestern starting offensive line poured out of one van, Coach Mercer, the offensive coordinator and athletic director, emerged from the other. The linemen were all wearing blue jeans and their jerseys. Mercer was carrying a small bag.

The coach shook Tony's hand, introduced himself and the rest of the group who all, in turn, shook his hand and congratulated him on his season. When the introductions were over, Mercer pulled out a purple number 9 Wildcats jersey with MICHAELS on the back.

"This is yours if you want it, and these fellas here," Mercer said, pointing to the offensive linemen "well, they would love to block for you next year. What do you say?"

"Absolutely!" Michaels shouted. He then raised his arms in the air, leaned back and let out a celebratory scream toward the sky.

After Michaels exchanged high fives with the offensive linemen, Coach Mercer gave Tony his card and asked him to call the next day to set up his official recruiting visit. The entourage then got back in their vans and pulled away. Michaels couldn't stop smiling.

That night, instead of researching schools, Michaels personally e-mailed every one of the coaches who had recruited him to inform them of his decision. Then he posted a YouTube video announcing it to the world.

Freshman year started with Tony Michaels on the bench and a returning senior as the starting quarterback. After losing the first three games, though, Coach Mercer decided it was time to let the young man with the cannon arm play. With Michaels leading the way, Northwestern finished 7–6, including a win in the Heart of Texas Bowl.

Sophomore season, Michaels led the Wildcats to a 9–4 record and a win over Auburn in the Citrus Bowl. Northwestern had been playing intercollegiate football since the late 1800s and had won a total of two bowl games prior to Tony's arrival, and now they had won back-to-back bowl games. Tony was becoming a celebrity in Chicago and drawing national attention.

Tony loved the attention, and he loved the opportunities to appear on sports talk shows. He would tape each appearance and analyze each one the same way he would analyze game film, looking for anything he could improve upon. He was always looking at how he looked at the camera, where he put his hands, how his smile looked. Any minute detail that Tony thought could be improved to make him look more polished would become a mission for him.

Going into his junior season, Tony Michaels was being mentioned as a Heisman Trophy candidate. It was an award no Northwestern player had ever earned. But the hype ended on the first drive of the season when Tony was hit low just as he was releasing a pass. The results of that play were a touchdown and a torn ACL. Tony's season was over and surgery was needed.

Without all the football commitments, it freed Tony up to take an internship with ABC 7 in Chicago. At first he was limited in what he could to, but he loved being in the newsroom. As his leg improved, he was allowed to go out into the field with reporters. Eventually, he did a few stories on his own. He loved being in front of the camera. And just as with the interviews, he analyzed all of his "game film" for ways to improve.

Tony's father passed away that summer from cancer, but it made him more determined than ever to be successful and to not live the difficult life his father had. He pledged to be better than ever, and he dedicated the season to his father.

With the leg completely healed, the next season Tony was ready to take back the reins of the Wildcat football team. Coach Mercer reluctantly agreed to allow Tony to continue his internship and even do "special reports" on the team for ABC 7 as long as it didn't interfere with football. Tony provided a unique look into the lives of college athletes and did special segments on teammates and coaches. The fans and viewers of Chicago loved it. So did the networks.

With Michaels back on the field, Northwestern appeared on national television often. Both ABC and ESPN would show the reports as part of their pregame shows. And despite Mercer's concerns of it becoming a distraction, Tony worked harder than ever on his game just to make sure he would be allowed to continue doing the reports.

The final results were a Heisman Trophy, a 13–1 season with a Big Ten championship and capped by a win over Oregon in the Rose Bowl. Tony's special reports with an inside look at the Heisman experience (which included a tribute to his father) and the Rose Bowl experience even won him a local Emmy Award and an ESPY, in addition to the one he received for best male college athlete. The Emmy was his favorite of his trophies.

Tony was surprised by how much he had grown to love the game. He wasn't surprised so much by the success, because he had worked his butt off to get it. Having been so heavily re-cruited, most around the country weren't surprised by what he was doing, but definitely surprised that he was doing it at Northwestern.

Having redshirted his junior year, Tony was ready to grad-uate, but still had one more year of eligibility. He had received a few job offers to be a reporter, a handful of offers to be an anchor in smaller markets and was being projected as a first- or second-round pick if he declared for the NFL draft.

Coach Mercer, who was a bit of a father figure to Tony be-fore his dad passed away, had become even more important in his life since. Coach Mercer was being rumored for several vacancies at more prestigious schools. When things had calmed down following the Rose Bowl, the two met for breakfast to discuss their options. It turned into an all-day conversation about a wide variety of topics.

When the draft finally came up, Coach Mercer told his quarterback that if he really loved football, he should declare for the draft. It would make him a millionaire. If he really loved the reporting he should go for that. Coach had seen how hard Tony worked at both and knew he would be successful at either. If he wasn't sure, he could always play one more year at Northwestern while he decided.

"What about you, Coach?" Tony asked. "I hear USC and Miami both want you. Think of how much better the weather is there. Think of how much easier it would be to recruit there. And I heard this morning on the radio that the Patriots may want you as an assistant coach."

Coach Mercer laughed. He told Tony that he hadn't really had time to think about it yet, but he would weigh all his options. Coach Mercer asked Tony to call him when he made his decision.

"Of course, Coach. As soon as I know, you're the first one I would tell anyway."

"Well, son, if you decide to stay, I'll stay, and maybe we win a national championship. Wouldn't that be something? Northwestern football winning a national championship?"

Tony knew that deep down, Coach Mercer really wanted to stay. Winning a national title at Northwestern would be a far greater accomplishment than doing so at USC or Miami. Plus, he had proven to be a great coach, and there would be plenty of opportunities the following season, national title or not. Tony knew how much it would mean to Coach Mercer, and he knew how much Coach Mercer meant to him personally. It was an easy decision to make.

Tony enrolled in a couple of graduate-level courses, but mostly he wanted to have fun, win some football games and relish in his last opportunity at the college experience.

When Tony announced his decision to return for his final season, Coach Mercer withdrew his name from consideration for other jobs and made a final push on recruiting before National Signing Day. All the recent attention, the bowl victories, Tony's Heisman and Coach Mercer's commitment to staying made Northwestern a much more appealing choice than it had ever been. The Wildcats hauled in what many experts called their best recruiting class in school history.

The university took out an insurance policy for Tony, a common practice at major football programs for star athletes, but this was another first for Northwestern. With Tony projected by most analysts to be the No. 1 overall pick in the draft heading into the season, the policy protected Tony in case of injury. There would be a payout if the injury knocked him out of the first round and another payout if he could no longer play football.

The decision to stay looked like it was paying off. Northwestern was 9–0 and dominating every opponent. The Wildcats were ranked No. 1 in the country, and Tony Michaels was on the verge of becoming only the second player in history to win the Heisman Trophy twice.

The Wildcats were a 22-point favorite against visiting Michigan at Ryan Field. It was 29 degrees at kickoff. Snow had been falling all morning, and the gusting wind brought the wind-chill factor into single digits.

Northwestern won the coin toss and elected to receive the kickoff. Tony quickly marched them down the field for a touchdown and a 7–0 lead. Michigan went three and out on its first possession and a bad punt set the Wildcats up at the Michigan 42 yard line. Ryan Field was rocking, and it appeared the rout would be on.

Coach Mercer decided to go for it and throw deep on first down, feeling another quick score would demoralize the visitors and the Wildcats could go into cruise control. Northwestern lined up with five wide receivers and Michaels in the shotgun. Michigan came with a blitz. On Tony's blind side, the left tackle slipped on the snowy field and fell. He grabbed his man as he was falling, bringing him to the ground with him.

The yellow penalty flag came out, sending up a small puff of snow when it hit the ground. Tony was looking to the slot receiver on the left side who had beaten his man. He was just about to release the ball when the blitzing linebacker came free from his right side and hit him squarely in the chest. Tony fumbled the ball, his feet went out from under him and he was flying backward. The linebacker was still on top of him when he landed, his outstretched arm came crashing down on the helmet of the Michigan defender who had been taken to the ground by the left tackle.

A hot jolt of pain went through Tony's right arm. He briefly fainted as players on both teams went after the fumble but the cold of the snow inside his face mask quickly brought him back. Tony's golden right arm felt like it was on fire, and he was unable to move it. Television cameras and most of the crowd were focused on the fight for the loose ball and did not notice their star player lying motionless in the snow. Blood was coming from his arm, forming an expanding red circle on the otherwise white field.

It was a Northwestern wide receiver who first noticed his fallen teammate as officials were scrambling to get to the bottom of the pile. He began waving wildly toward the sidelines for the trainers to come out when a Michigan player came out with the ball.

The huddle around Tony had grown larger than the mass of players around the ball. The crowd had gone silent. Michaels was going into shock. He briefly wondered if his arm was still attached to his body. Then he fainted again.

The next thing Tony knew, he was in recovery after the first of what would be three surgeries on his right arm. In addition to the compound fracture of his humerus, Tony had dislocated both his shoulder and his elbow. Doctors inserted a titanium rod to protect his humerus.

Tony's first words after surgery were "Did we win?" The nurse wasn't sure, but she said she would ask his coach. Northwestern had indeed gone on to win the game. None of the players had showered after the game. All had just changed quickly into street clothes and headed to the hospital. Showers could wait, their leader was in trouble.

Tony's mother and Coach Mercer were the first two allowed in when Tony was recovered enough to see visitors. They each visited briefly and promised to be back. Then one-by-one the entire Northwestern Wildcat football team popped in to give encouragement to their wounded leader, who had turned their program around and made them proud to wear purple. Even a few Michigan players had stayed behind to check on the Heisman winner.

When all the players were gone, Coach Mercer came back in.

"Tony, you're like a son to me," Coach said through tears. "Anything I can do to help, just holler. But I need you to get well enough to travel by bowl season. If we can win the National Championship, I want you to be the one to accept the trophy."

As Tony nodded, Coach added, "They want me to get out of here and leave you alone to rest, but I will see you tomorrow."

Coach Mercer would visit Tony in the hospital every day until he was released. Northwestern finished the regular season undefeated and won the Big Ten West Division, but lost to Ohio State in the conference championship game.

Northwestern went on to play Florida State in the Orange Bowl. When the team found out Tony would be able to travel to the game, they insisted despite not playing, he should be a captain and be the one to make the call for the coin toss.

When the Wildcats took the field for pregame warm-ups, every player was wearing No. 9 jerseys. The captains were introduced for the coin toss and as Tony's name was announced it drew a loud standing ovation, even though the majority of the crowd was wearing the garnet and gold of Florida State. With his right arm still in a sling, Tony waved in appreciation with his left hand and took it all in. The Seminole captains all gave him a hug and wished him well.

Tony called heads. The coin came up heads, and Northwestern took the ball. Tony's teammates were fired up to win this for their leader and took an early 14–0 lead in the first quarter before Florida State was able to settle into a rhythm and get back in the game.

In the fourth quarter, the Seminoles were leading 27–21 and driving when Tony's roommate, Northwestern senior safety Andy Patterson, intercepted a pass and returned it 97 yards for a touchdown to put the Wildcats back in front. The Northwestern defense needed to make one final stand, and Patterson stepped up again, blocking a Florida State 30-yard field goal attempt that would have won the game just as time expired.

It wasn't the national championship trophy but Tony went up on the podium with Coach Mercer to accept the trophy. With only one good arm, Tony wasn't able to lift the trophy, but he grabbed an orange with his left hand and held it high. His teammates went nuts. Tony wondered if this would be the last time he would ever be on a football field.

When he first wrote that letter to Coach Mercer, football was completely secondary. He was using it to get the degree he wanted from the school he wanted. The injury wasn't going to ruin his dream of being a news anchor. But football had earned a special place in his heart. He loved the game now, he loved his coach, he loved his team and he was going to miss it all.

Tony had needed a fourth surgery by the time the NFL's annual scouting combine rolled around. Before the injury, it had become a foregone conclusion that his would be the first name called in the draft. Now everyone wondered how long it would take before he could play again—or if he could ever play again.

With his arm in a sling, Tony attended the combine. Mostly just to take in the experience. There would be no workouts, no 40 times, but he wanted to be available for interviews if any teams or their doctors wanted to talk to him. Several team doctors spoke with him and reviewed his medical history. Several coaches came by to congratulate him on his career and a few teams actually interviewed him.

Tony left the combine pretty certain that he wouldn't be drafted. It wasn't too big a deal, because he had never dreamed about playing in the NFL. Still with all the hard work he had put into learning the sport and learning to play quarterback at such a high level, it was a letdown to think it would all be over. His roommate, Orange Bowl hero and fellow broadcast journalism major Andy Patterson, was also at the combine. Andy did well in all the workouts but was projected to be a late-round pick, at best.

By the time the draft rolled around, Tony still had very limited use of his right arm. He was getting used to doing things left-handed, but it had been a struggle. Tony was having dinner with his mother when his cell phone rang. It was the Dallas Cowboys calling to let him know he had been drafted.

Dallas knew Tony wouldn't be able to play that season, but they liked his game, and they loved his leadership. A trade with Cleveland had netted the Cowboys two extra picks in the seventh round. They took a chance and used one of those picks on the former Heisman Trophy winner.

A few minutes later, Tony's phone rang again. The Cowboys used their final seventh-round pick on Andy Patterson. The two would be headed to Dallas together.

Tony still couldn't throw a football when training camp

opened. But he worked as hard as he could on his physical therapy and anything he could do in the gym that didn't affect his arm. He memorized the playbook and helped as much as he could in practice. The coaches were impressed by the effort and rather than release Tony, they decided to place him on the injured reserve list. Tony couldn't help them right away, but the Cowboys figured it was worth it to keep him around another year. They also didn't want him to regain his Heisman form for somebody else.

Andy did everything he could to stand out in practice and in the preseason games. The Cowboys cut him, but offered him a spot on the practice squad.

Tony and Andy spoke daily and had dinner together regularly. They sometimes would reminisce about their Northwestern days and how crazy it was that they ended up in Dallas together. They were best friends, but their paths were so much different. Andy grew up always wanting to be a professional football player. It was the only dream he ever had. Northwestern was the only school to offer Andy a scholarship so he joined the Wildcats with a chip on his shoulder, determined to prove everybody wrong. He majored in broadcast journalism, thinking that after a long career in football he could land a job as a football analyst for one of the networks.

One Monday night when Andy was worried he would be released from the practice squad and Tony was considering quitting football the two went out for drinks. Tony was instantly smitten with their waitress Katherine, with her light brown hair, sparkling green eyes and gorgeous smile that made his heart skip a beat.

Dating had never been difficult for Tony. He was tall,

good-looking and a star quarterback—a pretty good formula for attracting women. But he had never met anyone like Katherine. With just a quick introduction and a little light banter he knew Katherine was special.

After a few beers, Tony got up the courage to ask Katherine out on a date.

"I'm sorry but I don't date my customers," she replied.

"I will leave right now and promise never to come back again," Tony offered with a smile.

Katherine just laughed and walked away. But as she walked away she turned back and flashed that smile again. Tony thought if he could see that smile enough, the pain in his once-golden right arm would surely go away.

When she came back to the table she had two more beers.

"This round is on me," she said. This time she threw a wink in with the smile. "Y'all can't leave. Y'all are my favorite table tonight."

As the night went on Tony and Katherine kept exchanging banter, and when Tony would go to the men's room, Andy would try to pump his buddy up. By the end of the night, Katherine had loosened her stance a little.

"You seem really sweet," she said. "I work the lunch shift tomorrow. I always get coffee across the street. If you are there at 9 a.m. I'll let you buy me coffee. If you buy me coffee I'll sit and talk to you and I just might give you my phone number so we can go on a date. But if you aren't there and I have to buy my own coffee, you'll never have a shot with me."

She smiled one last time. She knew she had him. Tony set three alarms for the next morning on his phone, and then called a cab. He was at the coffee shop by 8:30. Katherine walked through the door exactly at 9 o'clock.

Tony lit up when he saw Katherine. They said their hellos and ordered their coffees. They sat and chatted for about forty-five minutes until Katherine needed to head to work. She put her number in Tony's phone and said, "I'm free on Saturday night. You should call me tonight with how you plan to sweep me off my feet."

Katherine gave Tony a hug, and then left. Both were grinning ear to ear. Tony sent a quick text to Andy proclaiming, "I am going to marry our waitress from last night."

Tony was immediately inspired by meeting Katherine. Instead of giving up on his rehab and football, Tony decided to do everything possible to get his arm well enough to make the team the following season. And he decided that he would also get back to practicing his news broadcasts and start working on videos to send to local stations.

As the No. 5 media market in the country, Dallas was two notches below Chicago, but still plenty big enough. The weather was better, and Chicago didn't have Katherine. Dallas would work just fine. He made a pledge to himself that he would make the Cowboys the following season and if that didn't work out, he would be ready to land a TV job in Dallas.

With Tuesday being a day off for the Cowboys, Tony put together some of his videos from his days at ABC 7 in Chicago and sent them, along with a letter of introduction, to all the Dallas stations. The letter explained his situation, his ongoing attempt to play football, his ultimate goal of being an anchor for the national news and his willingness to do anything that did not interfere with his obligations and commitments to the Cowboys.

Then he called some of his teammates for advice on the best places in the Dallas area to take someone on a first date.

Tony called Katherine Tuesday night and they spoke for hours. They spoke every day until their date on Saturday. By the end of the week, every station in town had contacted Tony and wanted to meet with him so his confidence was growing.

The date went very well. As Tony was walking Katherine to her door he paused. "I hope I'm not being too forward," he said, trying to be a gentleman, "but are you free tomorrow?"

"I don't know," she answered with a smile that let him know it would be okay to see each other two days in a row. "I'm not working. I'll probably just watch the Cowboys game. Maybe see if the girls want to grab some drinks."

"Well, how about watching the game with me—at the stadium?"

"Really?" Katherine was beaming. "Absolutely!" she shouted before planting a good night kiss on Tony.

The two met at the coffee shop again the next morning. Tony took her down on the field before the game and introduced her to some of the players. Katherine confessed that as a little girl she dreamed of being a Dallas Cowboys Cheerleader.

"You would have been great," Tony said reassuringly.

Katherine laughed. "You haven't seen me dance."

"Well, I hope this lasts long enough that I get to see it," he answered.

The two went to their seats, watched the game, and chatted, laughed and smiled like they had known each other their whole lives. Neither said it, but both were thinking it would be great to spend the rest of their lives like this.

Andy was released by the Cowboys that week. But after some injuries the team signed him again and he was on the active roster for six games, appearing mostly on special teams.

Over the next few weeks, the relationship between Tony and Katherine blossomed. Tony met with several station directors. They all wanted him, some for just for sports, some for news. They all were impressed by his prior work and by earning an Emmy in a larger market than the Metroplex. But they all wanted more of a commitment than he could make while pursuing football. There was a mutual agreement to stay in touch.

Tony got the best feeling from Channel 9 news director Bob Dunham. Dunham assured him that a job was waiting for Tony when he was ready to take it. The two spoke regularly and developed a friendly, professional relationship.

The following summer at training camp, Tony failed his physical with the Cowboys. He had done everything he could to get the arm in shape. Overall, he was in the best shape of his life, but there was no zip on his throws. There was still pain and there was no way his arm would hold up to the rigors of the NFL. The Cowboys released Tony and wished him well. His first call was to Katherine. His second call was to Bob Dunham. Dunham officially offered him a job as a reporter, and they agreed on a start date. After that, he called his mother and Coach Mercer.

When the insurance payout came, Tony used the money to buy a house in Plano. He hadn't told Katherine about the insurance policy, and he wanted to surprise her with the house.

He told Katherine he wanted to take her on a picnic. She agreed. Tony made her put on a blindfold, then drove to the house. He led her through the gate into the spacious backyard. He had set up a chair in the backyard that morning. Katherine sat down, still blindfolded, while Tony set up the picnic.

When he was finished he took the blindfold off Katherine. She was delighted—but not surprised—to see the picnic included many of her favorite things.

"Where are we?" she asked.

"Just a nice backyard of a vacant house," Tony answered. "It seemed like a nice quiet place for a picnic, much better than a park with other people bothering us."

Katherine objected, worried that they would get caught and in some kind of trouble.

"Would it make you feel any better," Tony asked as he reached into his pocket and produced a key, "if this was your house?"

Katherine shrieked with joy. She was giddy and wanted to see the house immediately, but Tony convinced her they should eat first. Katherine ate quickly, not aware of the taste of anything, but cherishing the feeling of sun on her face and the joy in her heart as she finished the picnic with the man she truly loved. This was a moment she would never forget. She wasn't sure she would ever be able to stop smiling.

Katherine was in a hurry to see the house, but not in a hurry to leave the picnic. The backyard would never look exactly like it does now she thought. The tree would grow, the fence would fade, they might eventually paint the house a different color. She wanted to remember every detail as it was in that moment.

Tony got up, helped Katherine to her feet and took her on a tour of the house. Her house. Their house. She imagined making love by the fireplace, hosting dinner parties, and hopefully, someday having children and raising them in this house.

This was far too much house though, she thought. There was no way they could afford a house like this. Then Tony explained the insurance policy and how he had paid cash for the house and that he bought it with the hopes of it being their house, not just his.

Back downstairs, Katherine whirled with glee, then leapt into Tony's arms and planted a kiss on her love.

"I could never be happier than I am right now," she said.

"Are you sure about that?" Tony asked with a wry smile.

Katherine climbed down from Tony and stepped back, not sure how to reply to his query. Tony then silently knelt to one knee and produced a sparkling diamond ring. Katherine let out another shriek of joy, then tackled Tony to the ground and kissed him as passionately as she could.

When they stopped kissing, Katherine officially said, "Yes." Tony placed the ring on her finger and Katherine proclaimed, "We will be the happiest couple ever!"

"Agreed!"

Over the next few months, Tony put everything he had into his career. Katherine quit her job and her responsibility became furnishing and decorating the new Michaels household. Tony was building his contacts and sources. He never missed a detail when reporting on a story and worked hard to find stories where there were no obvious stories. The public began to love him, and most importantly, so did Channel 9 news director Bob Dunham.

Tony and Katherine were married in March the following year. When they returned from their honeymoon, Dunham asked Tony to fill in for longtime 6 o'clock anchor Kurt Jackson who was taking time off for a medical procedure. With Tony filling in as anchor, Channel 9 received its highest ratings in years, double the numbers from the same week the previous year. Jackson returned, but Dunham made the call that Tony Michaels was now the face of Channel 9.

Jackson finished out his contract working as a fill-in on weekends and on the Channel 9 morning show. Tony flourished in his new role. Never one to lack in confidence, Tony grew the more the spotlight shined on him. He continued to be hungry and was not content to just read the news, he still continued to report on and find stories as much as his anchor duties would allow.

Within three months of taking over as anchor for the 6 o'clock news, Tony Michaels was offered a substantial raise to also be the anchor for the 10 o'clock news. Channel 9 now had the two highest-rated news broadcasts in the state. That's when the billboards with Tony's face started to pop up across the Metroplex.

Tony and Katherine seemed to have the perfect marriage. Both were immensely happy and supportive of each other . . . until fate took its first swipe at the couple. The network's national news anchor announced his impending retirement. Tony received a call at work from the network asking him to fly to New York to discuss becoming the replacement. Tony Michaels was young, energetic, good-looking, charming, charismatic, intelligent and a brilliant reporter. He was everything the network could hope for.

This was the opportunity Tony had always dreamed about. Anchoring the national news was one of the few things he had ever wanted in life, except for Katherine and for a brief period of time to be quarterback of the Dallas Cowboys. The person Tony spoke to at the network assured him this was not an interview. Tony was the only candidate being currently considered. He was merely being beckoned to New York to make sure it was a good fit for him.

Tony came home that night happier than he had been since the day he proposed to Katherine. He couldn't wait to tell her the great news. The hard work had paid off. Being the national anchor at his age was unheard of, but the exposure and the pay would be his dream come true.

"We can't move to New York," said Katherine as she dropped the first bomb of the relationship. "I'm pregnant. I can't take my parents' first grandchild thousands of miles away and I don't want to raise a child in New York. I want to stay in Texas. I want to stay in this house. I want to raise our children in the house that you bought for us."

Tony and Katherine had never fought or even had a real argument until that moment. But the fight would continue for days. Katherine, who had never been outside the state of Texas except for their honeymoon, insisted on staying in their house in Plano, which was only three miles from her parents. Tony argued that this was his opportunity to fulfill a lifelong dream. Katherine's argument was that Tony should be content where he was. He was making a substantial salary already, and New York would be so much more expensive.

Katherine also didn't think New York was an ideal place to raise a child.

As the fight lingered, Katherine went to visit her parents. Tony called his old friend Andy Patterson who was still clinging on to his career with the Cowboys, mostly playing special teams, and the two went to Hooters. After a couple plates of wings and a few pitchers of beer, their waitress Taylor told the boys that she was being cut. She asked if they wanted their tab or to be transferred to the new waitress. The gentlemen agreed it was time for the check.

When Taylor dropped off their check, it had a lip print on it. A huge pink heart was around the total. At the bottom she had written in large pink letters "DTF?" She placed the bill right next to Tony to make her intentions clear.

Tony loved Katherine, but the fight had not been resolved. If she loved him, how could she hold him back from achieving his lifelong dream? In a moment of weakness as Taylor picked up his credit card, Tony said yes. He told her to add two more pints to the tab for them to drink while they waited for her to finish up.

Andy called a cab for himself. Tony followed Taylor home and broke his wedding vows. At the time, it made sense to Tony. He felt betrayed that Katherine would not be supportive of his dreams so betraying her by having sex with another woman was only fair. It was only after the sex, after a shower and on his drive home that it hit him what he had done.

Tony had to pull off the road. He stopped and wept, worrying that he had thrown away the best thing that ever happened to him. When he got home, Katherine was already back from her visit with her parents. Tony immediately broke down and confessed. There was another small fight, but Katherine insisted the two would work through this. They were meant to be she claimed. As long as Tony agreed to stay in Plano and not cheat again, there was nothing that could break them up.

Besides watching the news, Tony's favorite memories of his father were watching him do woodwork in their garage. Tony's parents didn't have much money, so Tony's father had learned carpentry on the side out of necessity. He could afford to make things that he could not afford to buy. Nearly all the furniture in Tony's childhood home had been built by his father. Others had been impressed by his work and for extra cash, Tony's father would occasionally build things for neighbors and friends.

When Katherine forgave Tony, he became inspired by this memory of his father. Tony wanted to build the crib and as many baby items as he possibly could. He went out and bought all the tools he thought he would need. For the rest of Katherine's pregnancy, Tony spent all of his free time either doting on his pregnant wife or in his new workshop crafting items for the baby.

By the time the baby arrived, the relationship had been more than repaired. It appeared to be thriving. Katherine insisted on naming the child Tony Jr., although he would spend much of his life being called TJ. Tony could not have been more thrilled. His focus now was on being the best husband and father he could be.

As happy as he was in that moment and as much as he loved Katherine, he hadn't forgotten about the New York opportunity. Katherine had forgiven him for his infidelity, but Tony had not yet forgiven her for crushing his dream. Their friendship was as strong as ever and their shared loved for TJ would always be a bond. Yet Tony wondered if things could ever be the same.

Things remained great for the first two years of Tony Jr.'s life. "Uncle Andy" had become expendable for the Cowboys, replaced by players who were younger, stronger, faster, hungrier and cheaper. He quickly found work on sports talk radio in Dallas. At best he was marginal as a football player, surviving more on heart than talent or ability, but he was a natural behind a microphone.

One of the local stations had a Cowboys show every Wednesday during the football season hosted on a rotating basis at the plethora of Hooters throughout the Metroplex. When Andy Patterson was asked to be the host of the show, he jumped at the opportunity.

As often his schedule would allow, Tony would stop by after the news and have a beer or two with his old friend. They had always been quick visits since his indiscretion.

Tony had been working so hard at his career that he hadn't taken a vacation since the honeymoon. He got an e-mail from the HR department informing him that he had maxed out his vacation time and he needed to take time off per company policy. He discussed vacation ideas with Katherine who preferred that he just stay home and spend extra time together. She suggested they take TJ to places like the zoo and the aquarium. She wanted to take a week to do all the fun things they often didn't do because they tried to avoid places that were too crowded.

The week started off great. The three were having a blast. But on Wednesday, Tony suggested going to see Andy do his show live. Since Tony was always working evenings, he hadn't had a chance to see his friend's show, only meet him later for drinks. Katherine really liked Andy, but she had no interest in going to Hooters. She told Tony to go and have a good time. TJ was worn out from the day at the zoo and had passed out on the couch. Katherine just wanted to relax at home.

Katherine kissed Tony on the cheek, smacked him on the butt and yelled in her best coachlike voice, "Now get out there and have some fun!" Tony kissed her back. She smiled, winked and said, "Tell Andy I said hi."

As Tony left, he had a warm feeling in his heart. Things had never been better, he thought. He needed to take more time off work to spend with his wife. He would have to look at the calendar and figure out the best time to go. He was hoping he could eventually talk Katherine into going to Hawaii or maybe one of the Disney parks. But if they just stayed home and played together that wouldn't be too bad either.

Tony arrived at the Hooters before Andy had arrived so he just grabbed an open table and was sending his friend a text when his waitress came bouncing to his side.

"Oh my God!" screamed his waitress Angelique when she realized the face of Channel 9 was sitting in her section. "You're Tony Michaels! I love watching you on the news! I can't believe you are sitting in my section! Can I get a picture with you?"

"Only if I can get a picture with you," said Tony coyly, finding himself strangely flirting. Since the one night of infidelity, Tony had been a rock. But the lovely Angelique was going to be his kryptonite.

Another waitress took their picture on both phones and walked away. "Do you mind if I post this on Facebook or

Instagram?" Angelique inquired politely. Tony simply nodded, finding himself mesmerized by Angelique's smile and dazzling blue eyes. He couldn't help but notice she had a spectacular body as well and deep down he loved it when she would flip her long, curly, blond hair in a flirtatious manner.

Tony ordered a beer and couldn't take his eyes off Angelique's butt as she walked away.

"Goddamn!" Tony said as quietly as he could. Then he repeatedly told himself to be strong.

Angelique had just started her shift. The restaurant was not yet busy so Tony was her only table. She returned with Tony's beer, sat down and began to tell Tony everything relevant about her life.

Angelique was a student at Southern Methodist University in her junior year and majoring in journalism. Her goal was to be a weather girl. She still thought the term meteorologist sounded silly for somebody who would be spending all summer telling people that Texas would be hot. As a young girl, Angelique had two ambitions: to be a Dallas Cowboys Cheerleader and to do the weather on the news.

When she was nineteen, Angelique made the squad as a Dallas Cowboys Cheerleader. But she found the demands of being a full-time student, a cheerleader and holding down a job to be too much. So when the season ended, Angelique decided that her dream had been fulfilled and did not try out again. Since she started working at Hooters, she had finished as first-runner-up in the Miss Hooters pageant and was on the cover of the Hooters calendar, which she talked Tony into buying.

Tony found Angelique to possess both an irresistible cuteness and a fiery sexiness. He had to work hard to avoid thinking about what she might be like in bed. He just smiled, drank his beer and listened to her story, feeling a schoolboy crush building as the words floated out of her mouth.

With Tony's beer getting low, Angelique stood up. "I'm going to get you a new beer. Do you want anything to eat yet?" Tony nodded and ordered some food.

When Angelique came back with Tony's second beer she asked if he had any advice for breaking into the business when she graduated.

"Well, I would be happy to have you as a guest at the station," Tony offered, not yet realizing the trouble he was getting himself into as he spoke. "If you want, you can watch the broadcast from the studio. Then I can show you around the newsroom and introduce you to everyone."

"Are you serious? You can *really* do that?" said Angelique, barely able to contain her glee. When Tony nodded, she shrieked, "Oh my God! You are the best!" She stood up, jumped with joy, then nearly tackled Tony off his stool when she went to hug him. When they were safely balanced again and in no danger of falling, she apologized. She was just so excited.

"No worries," said Tony.

"Thank you," said Angelique, who then leaned in and kissed him on the cheek.

Fortunately for Tony, Andy arrived to interrupt briefly before setting up for his show. The restaurant was beginning to fill up, and Angelique was getting busier. Tony couldn't take his eyes off of her. He wondered if banging his head on the table might break the spell Angelique had seemed to cast upon him.

He spent the next few minutes staring at a picture on his phone of Katherine and TJ at the zoo earlier that day. That helped him put things into perspective . . . momentarily. Andy started his show and for the next hour, everyone's attention was on that. Tony was relieved. Angelique had a large party sitting at the Texas table that was taking up most of her attention. She checked on Tony often but didn't have the time to sit and flirt except for smiles and winks.

By the time Andy's show was finished, Tony was feeling strong again. He waited patiently while Andy mingled with the rest of the crowd and stayed long enough to have one more beer with his old friend.

When Angelique brought the check, she asked again about Tony's promise to see the broadcast and the newsroom. Tony gave Angelique his number and told her to text him next week and he would set it up. He paid his tab and headed home to his beautiful wife.

Tony and Angelique exchanged several texts over the next few days until they set up a day for Angelique to visit the newsroom. Angelique tried to be flirty, but Tony stayed strong, sticking to just details about her visit. She was much easier to resist via text than in person.

His last text to her, the day before the visit, was "btw, be sure to bring your résumé tomorrow.":)

Angelique showed up at Channel 9 looking quite business-like in a new skirt suit which she purchased just for the occasion. The skirt was just long enough to look professional but short enough and tight enough to show off the goods. The jacket was very sharp and professional. She chose a white silk top that revealed a fair amount of cleavage. At work she had caught Tony staring at her a few times, and she wanted to make sure she kept his attention.

Tony showed her around the set and took her to his desk
where he explained various details about the job. He then went to
makeup to get ready for the broadcast. He introduced Angelique
to the cameramen and showed her where she should stand during the broadcast. She was fascinated to watch it live, just a few
feet away. It seemed so different and magical versus watching it
at home. The experience definitely reaffirmed her career choice.

After the broadcast, Tony introduced Angelique to the
rest of the news team, took her on a tour of the studio and introduced her to all the personnel behind the scenes who made
the broadcast possible. Her head was spinning. Lastly, Tony
introduced Angelique to Bob Dunham.

"It's a pleasure to meet you, Angelique," said the Channel
9 news director. "Tony has told me a lot about you. We have
an internship opportunity available, and based on what Tony
has told me, it is yours if you want it."

Angelique squealed with excitement. "Of course! Of
course! Oh my God! This is a dream come true."

Dunham extended his hand to welcome Angelique to
Channel 9. She wanted to hug him, but settled for a handshake. Dunham told her to stop in on Tuesday to fill out all
the paperwork and go over her schedule and responsibilities.

Tony walked Angelique out. She was still so excited she
could barely contain herself. She hugged Tony as tightly and as
enthusiastically as she could.

"Thank you so much," she whispered in his ear. "You're
the best. I really owe you for this."

The hug lingered, and then Angelique kissed him softly on
the cheek. She stepped back and her smile was electric. He could
see and feel the kryptonite. He wanted to take her right there.

He started to wonder if he had just made the biggest mistake of his life. He knew he was lying to himself that he was just "helping" an ambitious journalism student get her first big break. He took one last furtive peek at Angelique's cleavage, gave her another quick hug and said, "I guess I will see you Tuesday!"

Angelique smiled. She noticed the lipstick on Tony's cheek and wiped it off. "I can't wait!"

Tony watched as she turned and walked away. He knew he was in trouble if she continued to dress like that around him.

"Goddamn!" he muttered under his breath. "This was a bad idea."

The internship was for only two days a week. That allowed Angelique to continue to focus on her studies and keep her job at Hooters so she could support herself until graduation. On those two days, she was completely focused on her duties and impressing everyone at the station. She learned everything she could about all parts of the broadcast.

Between the 6 o'clock and 10 o'clock broadcasts, Tony and Angelique usually had dinner together. They became friends. Angelique kept her flirting to a minimum at the station, but she kept it up enough to make sure Tony stayed intrigued. She could feel him weakening.

Angelique was so impressive in her role that she was called into Bob Dunham's office just two months into her internship. Dunham was sitting on the front of his desk, looking very serious. He motioned for her to have a seat.

"Angelique, I've been watching you work and I have come to the conclusion that I made a mistake," he said as Angelique gasped and slumped back in her chair. "I shouldn't have offered you an internship, I should have offered you a job!"

Angelique perked back up.

"The only open position is production assistant," Dunham told her. "The pay isn't great, but it's a full-time job, you'll get benefits and you'll be an employee so it will be easier to move you up when other positions become available. And it will look great on your résumé. We'll do our best to accommodate your school schedule until you graduate. What do you say?"

"I'll take it!" Angelique said emphatically as she stood up. This time she wasn't going to settle for a handshake. She hugged Dunham excitedly, then left his office and ran to Tony's desk to tell him the good news.

"That's fantastic!" Tony replied. "We should celebrate! If you want we can go out for drinks after we wrap up the broadcast. Should I invite anybody else?"

Angelique tried desperately to hide how much she hated the last part of Tony's offer.

"No, I think it should just be the two of us," she replied. "I would have never had this opportunity if not for you. I just want to celebrate with you, if that's okay."

"Sure," said Tony. "I need to finish writing my script for tonight but think about where you want to go. It's your night, so wherever you want to go works for me."

Angelique was positively glowing. Or maybe that was just the kryptonite.

Tony did take Angelique out for celebratory drinks that night. He was really proud of the initiative she had shown and how much she had grown and learned in such a short time as an intern. Now that she was going to be there more,

Angelique asked a lot of questions about what it was really like at Channel 9. She had a taste, but didn't know if it would be different as an employee than as an intern. She had a lot of questions about the business. Tony did his best to answer all of them and assure her that she was going to be as successful as she wanted to be in this business.

"Hey," Tony said, changing the subject, "your birthday is next month. I've been trying to figure out what to get you. I don't know if you want to give me any hints, but is there anything you need or want?"

"Honestly?" she asked. Tony nodded.

"You. That's what I need," Angelique was finally throwing it all on the table. Tony hadn't been responding to her hints so it was time to be blunt. "What I want is for you to take me to a nice dinner, maybe Bob's or III Forks and then take me home and fuck me until the sun comes up."

"Wow," gasped Tony. "Angelique, sweetie, I don't think I have hidden very well—if at all—that I've wanted you since the first day we met. It's part of why I got you the internship and why I pushed Bob to hire you. I've loved the flirting and I want you. I really do.

"But," Tony continued, "I love my wife. She is a wonderful person, wife and mother. I cheated on her once, and I am afraid if I do it again, I would lose her forever and she would take my son away. I can't risk that. I'm so sorry."

"No worries," Angelique answered. "I get it. And I'm sorry if I was too forward. You have been a great friend and mentor to me, and I totally appreciate you as a person. I hope this won't change our friendship at all. And I think you are totally sexy, so I'm not sure I can stop flirting with you. Can you live with that?"

Tony nodded.

"So we're good?" Angelique asked.

"Yes, we're good."

"Well, we should probably get out of here," Angelique suggested. "Thanks for the drinks and thanks for everything."

There was a friendly hug and Angelique gave Tony one last kiss on the cheek and walked out.

Tony went home that night and made love to Katherine. Well, his body made love to Katherine, but he wasn't completely sure who his mind was making love to. He was completely torn. He still loved Katherine, but she had already held him back once in his career. She didn't understand his ambition. He knew Katherine would never leave Dallas. His career would never grow beyond what he had already achieved.

Tony thought Angelique was a lot like him. She was ambitious and driven. She had a goal and was going to do what it took to reach that goal. It reminded Tony of himself during his high school and Northwestern days. Plus she was sexy as hell. Tony had always been so sure of everything, but he was totally conflicted now. For the first time in his life he had no idea what to do.

Angelique went home that night and fantasized about making love to Tony. As she brought herself to pleasure she wanted to call Tony so he could hear her and they could connect as she was doing it. It wouldn't be the same as him being there with her, but it would be the next best thing.

Angelique didn't get what she wanted that night, but she did get some very important information from Tony. He had cheated on his wife before. She reasoned that meant the door was open to make him cheat again. And he finally admitted that he wanted her. That was the key. That meant he thought about her. She wondered how often, but that didn't really matter. What mattered was that he wanted her, and she wanted him. The opportunity was there for her to seduce him. It might still take some work, but she was going to get her man.

The next day Angelique did some digging to find out where Tony worked out. Once she found out, she immediately went and joined his gym. She skipped classes the following morning and waited outside the gym until Tony showed up, so she would know when he worked out and she could arrange to run into him while making it seem like just a lucky coincidence.

One of Angelique's friends called her a stalker. But Angelique imagined herself as more of a lioness on the hunt. She liked the idea of being a sleek, sexy lioness, and she was definitely ready to unleash herself on her prey.

She had already taken the bold step of asking Tony to bed, so this would be easy by comparison. She went in the gym, turned on her MP3 player and hit the elliptical. She watched Tony as he worked out, trying to figure out the best time to pounce. Soon, she worked herself into a good sweat and headed in his direction.

As Angelique approached, Tony hadn't noticed her yet. She was wiping sweat off her brow with her towel to hide her face when she "accidentally" bumped into him. The two exchanged small talk. Angelique was very convincing when she told Tony she had no idea he worked out there. She told him she just joined because now that she was working in television, she had to keep her figure. Angelique then suggested they work out together. She had mostly stayed in shape by dancing and doing cardio but wanted to add some strength training, and she wanted Tony to teach her.

They started meeting at the gym every day pushing each other in their workouts. There was definitely a connection, and every day, Tony could see more similarities between them. Every day, Tony's body was getting stronger, and every day his will was getting weaker.

At the end of every workout, they would say "see you at work." Tony would head to the locker room, shower at the gym and then grab lunch on the way to the station. Angelique would head home, shower at home, fantasize that Tony was in the shower with her, make herself lunch and head to work.

Angelique had been studying Tony, both at the gym and at work. She was learning which smiles and flirtations had the most effect on him. She could feel his willpower fading.

A few days before her birthday, at the end of an especially difficult workout, both were gasping for breath. Angelique saw the opportunity to strike.

"I've been thinking," she said between deep breaths, "we drive two cars here every day and then we drive two cars to work every day. We leave at the same time and take two cars home every day. It's bad for the environment. We should carpool."

Tony was catching his breath while Angelique spoke. He agreed it made sense so Angelique continued.

"And since we're carpooling, you could shower at my place," she said, picturing a lioness in her head taking down a zebra. "We could even shower together to save water, you know, for the environment."

She then flashed her best kryptonite smile, the one that Tony had always reacted to the most strongly. She could feel him weakening. She could picture the zebra going limp, and the lioness preparing to feast.

Tony finally admitted defeat. "Yeah, for the environment," he said with a submissive smile. He could no longer hold out. The lioness was victorious.

This time, there was no confession to Katherine. And for Angelique's birthday he gave her a diamond bracelet with a note that said, "I wish I could stay until dawn."

Once he finally caved, Tony fell hard for Angelique. He still loved Katherine, but he was surprised to find that he didn't feel guilty about Angelique. He spent a lot of time thinking about it. Maybe he and Katherine had been growing apart. Maybe he still harbored resentment about the missed New York opportunity. Maybe he and Katherine just didn't really have that much in common except for TJ.

Tony decided that he shouldn't worry about why he felt that way. He didn't want to hurt Katherine, but now that he had given in to Angelique, there was no way he was going to give her up. His normal routine became having breakfast with Katherine and TJ, then spending some quality time with them before heading to the gym.

Most of the time, Tony and Angelique would work out, sometimes they would skip it. Either way they always ended up at her place, and then barely made it to work on time. Tony would do the broadcasts and since they were carpooling, take Angelique home. Sometimes he would stay a while and sometimes go straight home to Katherine.

Angelique made Tony feel more alive than he had ever felt. Maybe she was his soul mate. But, how could he ever break that to Katherine? Was Katherine sensing anything was happening? If she was, she hadn't let it show yet.

With Angelique around the station more, Bob Dunham

came to what should have been an obvious conclusion. As well as she had been doing at every assignment or task she had been given, it was obvious that Angelique had been born to be in front of the camera and not behind the scenes. While Tony and Angelique tried to hide their affair, there was obviously chemistry between the two of them.

As Channel 9 news director, Dunham even considered making them coanchors. He knew it would cause a stir among other reporters at the station, but it would cause a ratings spike for sure. He decided to play it cautious though and started giving Angelique feel-good and human interest stories that would build her confidence in front of the camera, provide her with more experience and give him more of a reason to move her into the anchor chair down the road.

Angelique also started doing the weather on weekend newscasts. And she was a natural. The weekend ratings did spike once Angelique made the move and it became obvious that Dunham couldn't hide her for long on weekends or on fluff stories. He had to move her into the regular news team, either on weather or as anchor. It was going to be a tough call to get rid of somebody, but the talent was there, and Angelique had an electricity that nobody else at Channel 9 had, not even Tony. Angelique was simply going to have to replace Tony on some of those billboards around the Metroplex.

Everything had been going perfectly between Tony and Angelique for months. If Katherine was suspicious, she wasn't showing it or no longer cared. The only thing Angelique wanted was more. She wanted weekends, she wanted Tony to stay the night. Wanting to keep Angelique happy, Tony began looking for broadcasting conventions or anything remotely work-related for excuses to spend a weekend with her. It was even better when he could convince the station to pay for the trips.

After returning from a trip to Vegas, the two had never been closer.

"I think you should get a divorce and marry me," she said matter-of-factly as he carried her luggage into her apartment. "I think you want that too. Actually, I know you want that. Why keep pretending?"

"It's not that simple, honey," Tony said apologetically. "I wish it was."

"You know it's the right thing to do," Angelique countered, flashing her best kryptonite smile. "And you know I always get my way. Why put off the inevitable?"

Tony kissed her.

"I love you," he said, not realizing at the time it was the first time he had said it out loud to any woman besides Katherine. "Angelique, I love you with all my heart and soul, but it's not that simple. We both need some rest. Can we talk about this some other time?"

"Okay," she said as she gave Tony a warm embrace. "But you know I'm right."

They held the embrace tightly for a few minutes, neither wanting to let go.

Finally Tony let go. "I need to get home, but I will see you in the morning. We'll talk about this another time, okay?"

Angelique nodded and gave Tony one final kiss good night.

The next day Tony was late picking Angelique up to go to the gym. He had never once been even a minute late for anything with her. He sent her an apologetic text and let her know he was on his way. "No worries," she replied. But what she meant was that he had better have a good excuse.

Tony arrived shortly. Angelique was naked when she answered the door and she jumped into his arms. "Let's skip the gym and call in sick to work," she whispered as she bit his ear. "I want to spend all day naked in bed with you."

Tony's response was less than enthusiastic.

"Sweetie, we need to talk."

Tony knew those words were never good words to say. Especially when the woman you love is naked and trying to seduce you. But they really did need to talk. Angelique jumped down and started cussing. He had never seen her mad before, probably because he had always given in to everything she ever wanted to that point.

She stormed into her bedroom, threw on a robe and returned. Tony was a little scared. The fire that made Angelique such an amazing lover was obvious, but that fire was being redirected into anger. He felt her stare burning his skin. There was no smile and no kryptonite, but Tony had never felt weaker than he did now.

"Okay, talk!" Angelique had never been short with Tony. Until that moment everything she said seemed to have a lyrical quality to his ears.

"Katherine is pregnant," Tony blurted out, getting right to the point. Angelique started pacing around the apartment.

Tony watched silently, hoping she would cool off. But the heat in the room kept building and the silence was growing oppressive. Finally Angelique shattered the silence, her lamp smashing into the floor. Tony watched the pieces fly through the air as though Angelique had just smashed his heart. A few sparks came out of the lamp and lit Angelique's rug on fire. Tony rushed to the kitchen, grabbed the fire extinguisher and put it out before it got bigger.

Angelique collapsed onto the couch. "How could you do this to me?" she asked. "How could you do this to us? Everything was perfect . . . and now *this!*"

Tony wasn't sure how to react. He was scared and now crying. He sat down next to Angelique on the couch hoping he could comfort her. She buried her face in his chest and wept.

When Angelique finally got her composure back, she kissed Tony, and then said, "I love you, Tony. And I am sure we will get through this, but right now I need you to get the fuck out and do not try to talk to me until I decide I'm ready."

Tony nodded silently, kissed Angelique on the cheek and headed out. After crying in his car for about fifteen minutes, Tony decided to hit the gym, hoping it would clear his head. He got on the treadmill and began running with Korn blaring through his earbuds. He couldn't get the image of Angelique as she smashed the lamp out of his head. He tried running faster. Nothing. Faster still. Nothing. Even faster, and then everything went black.

Tony awoke on a gurney, surrounded by paramedics. Combined with the emotions of the day, Tony had pushed himself too far. He was dehydrated and collapsed. He hit his head hard on the console of the treadmill on the way down, splitting his forehead open. A lady on a nearby treadmill immediately called 911, shut off his treadmill, grabbed his workout towel and applied pressure to his forehead attempting to stop the bleeding.

Tony had been unconscious for twenty minutes but had

been breathing fine and his vitals were normal. His head had already been bandaged, and the paramedics had started an IV and prepared him to be transported to the hospital. One of the paramedics said something to him, but Tony couldn't make it out. His forehead was throbbing so ferociously that it drowned out the man's voice. He was oblivious to almost everything around him.

At the hospital, Tony was checked out thoroughly. He underwent a CT scan, a neurological examination and cognitive testing. Tony was diagnosed with a Grade 3 concussion. The cut to his forehead did not require stitches, and the doctor assured him that he wouldn't have any scarring. The doctor also told him he would need to be off work for at least a couple weeks. By the time he was back, his forehead should look like nothing ever happened.

While Tony was running feverishly on the treadmill, Angelique got busy calling the other stations in the Metroplex to see if there were any positions available. There were no current openings, but the station managers were aware of her star power and were looking for ways to bring her on board.

While Tony was undergoing his CT scan at the hospital Angelique received a call from the Channel 6 news director. When he heard Angelique was looking for work, he fired one of the hosts of their morning show just to clear a space for her. He offered Angelique more than double what she was making at Channel 9 and assured her there would be opportunities later to move into the evening broadcasts for news or weather if she wanted them, but this was the best way to get her on board.

Angelique then went down to Channel 9 to speak to Bob

Dunham and quit her job. While she was waiting for Bob to get out of a meeting, she walked by Tony's desk, wanting to tell him first. Surprised he wasn't there, Angelique asked where he was. Somebody told her Tony had called in sick, which was unusual. He had never taken a sick day since starting at Channel 9. Later Bob informed her of what happened to Tony. Suddenly she felt sick.

It was difficult for Angelique to quit Channel 9, but she had to do it. The offer was too good to pass up. Bob was pissed when she told him, but he understood. He was mostly mad at himself for not promoting her sooner and making her the face of Channel 9, with a salary that other stations would not have been able to match. He shook Angelique's hand and wished her well, but once she was gone he threw a fit in his office.

One of his biggest stars was in the hospital, and he had just let the rising star walk out of his station. It was a dark day for Channel 9. He could feel the ratings slipping already and after being the number one news station for years, he suddenly felt concerned about his job.

Tony called Katherine when he was discharged. Katherine called Andy to help drive Tony's car home and help her get Tony home and into bed. He slept for the better part of the next three days. By Friday he felt well enough to go downstairs but not well enough to go back up so he slept Friday night on the couch. He spent a lot of time staring at his phone hoping to get a call or text from Angelique but his phone remained silent.

After one week, Tony was feeling close to normal except for the persistent headaches. After two weeks, he was better, but still had symptoms. After three weeks, his doctor wouldn't clear him to return to work unless it was only part time and only one broadcast per day rather than two. Bob Dunham agreed to limit Tony to just the 6 o'clock broadcast. He was just happy to have him back as ratings had suffered in his absence.

Tony returned to find that Angelique had quit Channel 9. She decided that she could no longer work with him. She couldn't walk past his desk and see his pictures of Katherine and TJ anymore. She wanted Tony for herself, and she couldn't be around any reminders that she was less than his everything.

Tony struggled through his first broadcast, but it felt good to be back where he belonged. As he got into his car, he received a text message. It was from Angelique.

"Not ready to talk. But saw you back on the news. Glad you're OK."

Eventually Tony would return to normal but the suits at Channel 9 decided to limit him to just the 6 o'clock news to lighten the load on him. It was partly for his health, but partly because they could see him slipping. When he first became anchor, he spent as much time as he could in the field reporting. Lately, he had become much less of a reporter and more somebody who simply read the news. He still did that very well. With Tony at the anchor desk, Channel 9 dominated the time slot and was still comfortably number one overall. But they thought by limiting his responsibilities he would take the initiative to get back to his old self.

Angelique was excelling in her new role. Doing the morning show was never what she had intended to do. The schedule was a tough adjustment, but it was an opportunity to shine. She was determined to shine so hard that Channel 6 would give her what she wanted. The lioness would not be tamed into doing the morning show for long.

She would still go to the gym, but it wasn't the same. Sometimes at night she would watch Tony on the Channel 9 news and feel a mixture of anger and sadness. He was a brilliant anchor, but he was also a great friend and a fantastic lover. The pain hadn't stopped since the day she kicked him out of her apartment. Her new job with the accompanying pay increase and growing celebrity status couldn't bring her anywhere close to the joy she felt with Tony.

So she finally broke down and sent a text. "I miss you." It was the longest minute of her life until she heard her phone beep. "Me too."

The two met for lunch the next day. At first it was awkward. The first few minutes were spent in a weird sort of argument over who could apologize more. When it was finally agreed that they both accepted some of the blame and both accepted the other's apology and wanted to move forward, they ordered lunch and enjoyed the rest of the afternoon together as friends.

When it was time for Tony to head to work, Angelique said, "You know I still want more, right?"

"Of course," said Tony. "We'll talk soon."

Tony and Angelique slowly rebuilt their friendship. With completely different schedules and now working at different stations, there were fewer opportunities to get together. And since Katherine's pregnancy, Angelique wondered if she had been a fool all along. She wanted to run as fast as she could into Tony's arms, but she held back, afraid that the new baby would just draw them farther apart. The lioness sensed danger so she proceeded with caution.

They texted regularly and had lunch occasionally. Angelique could see the hurt and loneliness in Tony's eyes. The lioness refused to let him see it in hers. It was there, but she restrained herself, wanting to be certain her heart wouldn't be broken again.

Three days before Christmas, an ice storm hit Dallas. Katherine's father had slipped on the ice while going out to get the newspaper. He had broken his hip and his wrist. He would be in the hospital for a few days and would need lots of care following his release.

Katherine decided that even though she was only a few minutes away, it would be better if she stayed with her mother, to keep an eye on her and drive her to the hospital and back. She packed some things, gave Tony a big hug and said, "I'm only a few minutes away if you need me," before helping TJ with his winter coat and heading out.

Tony spent the next couple of days alone with his thoughts, seeking perspective and trying to figure out what he really wanted. He spent Christmas Day at Katherine's parents' house. Tony had bought a present for Angelique, but she was spending Christmas with her family. When TJ fell asleep, Tony headed home to his solitude. Katherine stayed behind.

Katherine's father was released from the hospital, but he was in rough shape. Her mother wasn't going to be able to handle it alone so Katherine offered to stay at least another week. Which meant another week of solitude for Tony.

He sent a text to Angelique: Do you have a date for New Year's?

Not yet. Are you asking me?

Yes

OK, but on two conditions

What are they?

1. We stay in. I don't want to be at a big party. I want to be alone with you by the fire. We can either make dinner together or get takeout.

No problem. What's the other condition?

2. You have to spend the night with me.

Okay.

New Year's Eve was on a Friday. Tony spent the rest of the week in quiet contemplation. He faked his way through his broadcasts. By Friday, he was getting butterflies in his stomach. He was excited to see Angelique again. He was really excited to see her naked again, which hadn't happened since Katherine found out she was pregnant. There was no real news that day, and it was the most painful broadcast of Tony's life. He kept staring at the clock, which seemed to be moving far too slowly.

Finally it was time to sign off. Tony felt giddy. He called Katherine to wish her a Happy New Year and see if she knew when she would be home. Katherine had arranged for a nurse to help with her father. The nurse would be starting Monday, so she would be home then.

He rushed to Angelique's apartment, stopping to get flowers. At the flower shop, he realized he forgot her Christmas present at home, so he called Angelique to tell her he forgot something. Angelique said she would just order pizza and joked that Tony better get there before the pizza or she would have sex with the delivery guy instead. Tony sped home, grabbed Angelique's present and an extra set of clothes, then raced to Angelique's. With Katherine gone until Monday, he was hoping to get at least two nights with Angelique.

Angelique was excited by the flowers, and Tony beat the pizza guy by about five minutes. She joked that she meant what she said about banging the pizza guy, put the flowers in water, grabbed two cold beers and told Tony to go start the fire. Once the fire was lit and the pizza arrived, the two sat together on the couch watching a movie, smiling and laughing the whole time, occasionally stealing a quick kiss as the night progressed.

When the movie was finished, they cleaned up from dinner, and Angelique grabbed a couple of fresh beers.

"You know, I still haven't given you your Christmas present," Tony said coyly.

"You didn't have to get me anything," Angelique said, although she clearly perked up at the idea. "You being here is good enough for me."

Angelique kissed Tony like she used to kiss him when they first started seeing each other. Tony reached into his pocket and produced her present. Angelique slowly unwrapped her gift. There was a quick gasp when she saw the heart-shaped diamond necklace.

"It's beautiful. I love it!" she shouted, quickly turning around and demanding, "Put it on for me."

Tony put the necklace on Angelique, leaned in and whispered into her ear, "You will always have my heart."

Angelique smiled a huge smile. Not one of the smiles that she used to make Tony melt. This was a smile of smug satisfaction. The lioness was finally feasting on zebra again, and it felt wonderful.

Angelique walked over to a mirror to admire her new bauble. She turned around delighted with the gift.

"It's exactly what I wanted! In fact, it is so perfect that I am not going to wear anything besides this necklace until you leave," she said as she slipped her arms out of the dress and let it slide down to the floor.

She grabbed Tony by the hand and led him to the bedroom. The lioness was going to get her fill tonight.

In the morning, Tony informed Angelique that he could stay at least one more night. She didn't say a word, just smiled. Tony thought he hadn't seen her that happy since the first day they met at Hooters.

The two spent most of Saturday in bed, intermittently having sex, watching college football and taking naps. Angelique suggested they spend Sunday the exact same way, except for watching NFL instead of college. Tony thought it was a fine suggestion.

Tony wanted to stay Sunday night, but Angelique had to get up too early for her job hosting the morning show. So once the Cowboys had won their game and clinched a playoff berth, she told him to go. But unlike the last time she had thrown Tony out of her apartment, she kissed him passionately to let him know she really didn't want him to leave.

Tony went home to one more night of solitude and contemplation. He had to figure this situation out quickly.

Tony was awakened by an early phone call. He figured it would be Katherine probably to tell him she would be home shortly. But it was a network executive. The lead anchor in Los Angeles had announced he would be retiring when his contract was up in May. The network wanted to put a fresh face in the Los Angeles market and was checking in with some of the top anchors around the country to gauge their interest.

Tony was definitely interested. The executive told him that interviews likely wouldn't begin until March. At this time, they merely wanted to compile their list, and then evaluate all the candidates on their broadcasts and ratings over the next several weeks. After that evaluation, the list would be narrowed to two or three candidates who would be flown in for interviews. Based on what he had seen of Tony, he told him things looked promising to make the cut as long as nothing got in the way.

Tony was excited at first, and then dread hit him. He knew Katherine would react the same way she did when the New York opportunity arose. It hit him that Katherine would never let him leave Dallas. He would be stuck here in Dallas—forever. He had been number one in the ratings since he first took over, and he needed a new challenge, a new opportunity and a change of scenery. He could never get that with Katherine.

When Katherine returned, Tony didn't bother to mention the phone call. Tony tried not to show it, but the anger over the New York job was back. The two barely spoke at all. Tony spent all morning talking to and playing with TJ. He ate lunch in silence and then drove to work. Tuesday was more of the same.

Wednesday was a day off work for Tony. The Dallas Stars played almost all their games on Fox Sports Southwest, but Channel 9 had rights to ten games each year. Wednesday was one of those nights. A 5:30 local start time for a game at the Montreal Canadiens meant there would be no 6 o'clock news.

With the Cowboys in the playoffs, that meant Andy had at least one more week to do his show. Tony figured he could use a few beers with his old friend. But first he wanted to spend time with Angelique. He sent a quick text. "Do you want to have lunch?"

"Are you asking because you want lunch or sex?" :-)

"Lol, sex. But I was planning to buy you lunch first."

"K. I will call you when I am heading home" :-)

Tony and Angelique had a quiet lunch, and then made love passionately. They were curled up in bed, Angelique caressing Tony's chest. The lioness was happy. If Angelique could purr she would be purring. Tony noticed she was wearing both the necklace he gave her for Christmas and the bracelet he gave her for her birthday.

He wanted to have a serious discussion with Angelique, but didn't know how to bring it up. The lioness sensed he was troubled. She sat up and what she imagined as purring stopped.

"What's wrong, babe?" she asked.

Tony let out a huge sigh. "Nothing is wrong with us," he promised. "But something is bothering me, and I don't know what to do."

"Just tell me, sweetie, maybe I can help."

Another huge, full-body sigh, and then one more sigh that was only slightly smaller came from Tony before he could spit out his question.

"How big of a dick would I be if I ask my pregnant wife for a divorce?" he said in a defeated tone.

"Truthishly?" Angelique said with a smile and laughter. It was a made-up word she had stolen from a *Family Guy* episode. She liked to say it to break things up when the mood was too serious. The word always made her smile, and she wasn't going to make any effort to hide her joy at the thought that Tony was considering a divorce.

Tony went on to explain the phone call he got earlier in the week. He explained the previous experience with the New York offer. He explained that he felt he had accomplished all he could accomplish in Dallas and that he needed to reboot his life. He didn't see any way Katherine could be part of Tony 2.0. When he finished, there was another sigh.

"Honestly, and I'm being totally serious here," Angelique began her reply. "From the outside world, you will look like a gigantic dick. Everyone will think you are an asshole, and you will have to leave Dallas if you want to stay in this business, because I think ratings will suffer and Bob will fire you.

"But fuck everyone else," she continued. "They don't know you, and they don't know your situation. If they knew, they would totally be on your side."

Angelique was on a roll, her rant was just beginning. Her voice was growing louder. It was time for the lioness to roar.

"I've met Katherine, and she is beautiful. She is very sweet, and she seems like an excellent mother. I don't want to say anything bad about her because I know you loved her enough to marry her, but she is absolutely the wrong person for you.

"She has no ambition whatsoever, and she is a THREAT to your ambition. She doesn't support you AT ALL! She has already killed one amazing opportunity. She will kill this one, and she will kill every opportunity that comes along until she kills your soul. She is poison for you. I don't know what she was like before, but either she has changed, or she was like this all along and you just couldn't see it before because you were blinded by love. But there is no chance you will ever be happy if you stay with Katherine.

"I know you love your son and will probably love the

next kid just as much. But do you want your son to grow up in a relationship that is loveless and a complete lie? Or do you want him to know that it's not okay to stay in a dead relationship and that your love for him and Katherine's love for him will never weaken and may even be stronger once you are both free of the burden of being with the wrong person?

"I'm not saying this for me. I promise. I admit, if you do actually get divorced I'm not fucking waiting around. I am going to ask you to marry me. And if you're not ready, that's okay. And if it's not me, that sucks, but it will eventually be okay too. But if you stay with her, everything that is wonderful about you will die. And you will setting an awful example for TJ."

Angelique had finally let it all out. She was spent. Exhausted, she lay back down next to Tony, and she cried quietly. Tony just held her. When Angelique calmed down, she apologized.

"Don't," Tony said softly. "I asked you to be honest, and you were honest. And everything you said was true. I know it wasn't easy, but thank you."

Angelique had stopped crying and wiped the last of her tears away. Tony kissed her gently.

"If I get the LA job, would you move with me?" he asked. "I know you would have a job waiting for you out there if they know you're on your way. You would probably make more than me."

Tony was glad that Angelique was now smiling.

"Of course I would move to LA with you," she said.

"Okay," said Tony. "What if don't get the LA job? I don't know how much the divorce will cost me, but it will cost me a lot of money. I think I should still have enough that we could move a lot of places and take time to settle in before finding work. But I do think I need to leave Dallas one way or another."

"Just promise to take me with you wherever you go and I will be happy," Angelique requested.

"Deal," he answered. "You know, to be honest, I'm not sure I want the LA job. Maybe I don't want to be a news anchor any more. I'm not sure what I would do. Maybe I could become a broadcasting professor or coach football."

"I think you would be a wonderful professor and an excellent football coach," Angelique said supportively. "And who wouldn't want to hire a professor with your Emmy collection or a football coach with a Heisman Trophy? Personally, I don't care what you do as long as you stay true to yourself and do what makes you happy."

Tony kissed her with all the energy he had, looked deeply into Angelique's blue eyes and said, "You make me happy."

The lioness smiled, but she did need to remind her love that she was a lioness and she wanted this feast to last forever.

"This probably makes me a hypocrite," Angelique said, sliding her hand down to his crotch. "Especially since I have been the other woman. But this is mine. I want you all to myself. No lying, no cheating. Just me and you, loving and honest and happy. Can you promise me that?"

"Yes."

"Good," she said, climbing on top before one last ride. They fell asleep in each other's arms. Angelique woke up and looked at the clock. She nudged Tony awake.

"You should probably get out of here if you want to go to Andy's show."

"Maybe I want to stay here with you," he said with a smile.

"No, I need sleep, and you need time with your friend," Angelique smiled back. "And a few beers wouldn't hurt. You've had a rough day. But I will take a shower with you because you probably don't want to go to Hooters smelling like you do right now."

In the shower, Tony had one last question.

"Like you said, if I ask for the divorce now, Bob probably fires me which means the LA job is probably gone. So do I do it now or wait until after I find out about the job?"

"Well," Angelique said pausing to contemplate her answer, "I guess it depends if you really want the LA job and if you're really willing to wait until May to be happy. It might be harder after the baby is born though. As long as you keep the promise you made to me, I will support you, no matter what you decide. But if I get a vote, the sooner the better."

Tony arrived at Hooters at the same time as Andy. He offered to help set up.

"You okay, bro?" Andy asked. "You don't seem like yourself."

"I'll be fine," Tony replied. "I've got a lot on my mind, but don't worry about it now. We'll talk after the show."

"Anything you need, man," Andy said. "Just let me know. I've got your back."

Tony took a seat at a table. His waitress was beautiful, but unlike many other times, Tony didn't seem to notice. She introduced herself as Greta, but Tony was lost in his own mind and didn't catch her name, just as he didn't notice her long, dark brown hair or her lovely, welcoming smile that would have made him feel warm on almost any other day. Greta tried to engage him in conversation, but Tony wasn't really present yet. She had a fun, energetic personality, but it wasn't rubbing off on Tony.

He apologized and said maybe he would be more talkative after a beer or two. He also ordered some wings. Greta returned with his beer and a shot of Patrón.

"I didn't order this," he said.

"I know," Greta said, smiling and pointing toward Andy. "That guy bought it for you. He said you needed it."

"He's probably right," Tony answered with a smile. He raised his glass toward Andy and drank the shot. Greta left to check on another table. Tony was deep in thought. He kept replaying in his head what Angelique had said to him in the shower. He didn't want to wait until May to be happy. He wanted to be happy now.

He started to imagine waiting tomorrow morning at Channel 6 for Angelique to finish her show, and then just leave town right then. He had no clue where they might go or what they would do when they got there, but it would be an adventure, and it would definitely be fun. He knew deep down that Angelique was the right one for him. He wanted to start his life with her as soon as possible.

Tony didn't figure Katherine would still be awake when he got home, but he was going to tell her in the morning. Once that was over, he was going to quit his job. On his way to Hooters, Tony had seen two of the Channel 9 billboards with his image proclaiming him as "The Most Trusted Man in Texas."

Wow, that was one Texas-sized lie right there. The media was going to have a field day with this. "The Most Trusted Man in Texas" leaving his pregnant wife for a former Hooters calendar girl. It wouldn't matter why he was leaving Katherine. It wouldn't matter how great Angelique was, how real their love was, or anything else. They had met at Hooters, she had seduced him. Because of that, every time he went on the air and every time somebody drove by his billboard he was telling a lie.

Angelique was right. The sooner the better.

Tony didn't really listen to Andy's show. It was merely background noise as he practiced in his head how he would break the news to Katherine. The imagined conversations never went well. Tony knew the actual conversation would probably be worse. He didn't even notice when Greta brought his wings. She waved her hand right in front of his face until he finally blinked.

"If you don't cheer up, I will be forced to be obnoxious," Greta said with a not-so-serious voice, but a very stern look. "This is Hooters. You are supposed to be having fun! You're making me look bad."

Tony laughed and finally came back to the present. Tomorrow would have to wait until tomorrow.

"That's better," Greta said. She gave him a wink as she walked away. This time he noticed that she had quite a nice figure as well. But he snapped himself out of it and turned his attention away from her. He had enough problems in his life. He didn't need to start flirting with another waitress.

Tony ate his wings, drank his beer and made sure to smile occasionally. He watched the Stars game to keep his mind occupied and talked a little hockey with Greta. The Stars went on to beat Montreal in a shootout.

Andy finally joined him after the show was over and the

crowd had died down. Tony shared everything that had happened recently. Andy was blown away.

"I hate to see you leave, brother," Andy said. "I really hate to see you and Katherine split up, but Angelique is right. You're making the right decision. It sucks, but it's right."

"You would make one hell of a coach," Andy continued. "As far as professor, I'm not sure I would have graduated if it wasn't for you so any school would be lucky to have you. Anything you need from me, just holler."

The two stayed until last call when Andy ordered more Patrón. Tony shouldn't have driven, but he somehow made it home. The stairs were a challenge. When he reached the top, he noticed the room was beginning to spin. How much did he have to drink? He raced to the bathroom and threw up violently. He thought he was finished, but waited in case a second wave hit. He held on to the toilet as the bathroom seemed to swirl around him.

Finally, Tony got up, staggered toward TJs room, peeked in and saw him sleeping. He then staggered to his own bedroom. Katherine was still asleep. That was good news. He wondered if it was wrong to get into his own bed next to her, knowing what was going to happen in the morning. It all became moot as the room started spinning again. He lay down on the floor and grabbed the carpet as tight as he could, hoping that would help slow the spinning.

Tony woke up in bed. He didn't remember getting off the floor. He had a brutal hangover. He rolled over to look at the clock and was shocked when he saw it was 1:17 in the afternoon. Holy crap! He had never slept this late before. Even with his part-time schedule Tony had to be at work by two. He took a very quick shower and decided he could shave at the station. He always kept an electric razor in his desk just in case. There was no sign of Katherine or TJ. He figured Katherine had set up a playdate or had just taken him to Stonebriar Mall to play there or perhaps to her parents to check on her dad.

He threw on some clothes, grabbed his shoes and headed out. When they were first married, Katherine would always leave a note and often a snack if she left. If he had been drinking too much she would get TJ out of the house and let Tony sleep in quiet. The notes were always very sweet. Sometimes she even made lunch for him. But he was sure there wouldn't be a note or lunch today. He didn't deserve it anyway.

Tony walked out his front door and saw that he had parked next door in the Colemans' driveway. It was a good thing the Colemans were on vacation he thought, but he couldn't believe he was that drunk and made it home. He felt lucky and grateful to be alive. He also felt stupid for not calling a cab. Now that he didn't have the time, he was also glad his car was at least in the vicinity of the house.

He got to the station just in time for the 2:00 meeting. He looked like somebody who just woke up.

"You look like shit," Bob Dunham snarled. "Do you need somebody to cover for you tonight?"

"No," said Tony. "I'll have an energy drink or two from the vending machine and be ready to go by six."

Bob snapped. "Well, you better get your shit together soon. How are we supposed to stay number one in the ratings if you can't take this seriously? You stagger in late like you just came straight from the bar, looking like hell. You're better than this, Michaels. You're setting a terrible example for this team. I should send you home right now and make you personally take down all those billboards."

"I apologize, sir," Tony said. "There's a lot going on. I promise I will have it together when we go on the air."

"Well, you had better," Bob hollered. "We've been losing a lot of our lead lately, and I'm not going to give up that lead. You, of all people! Unbelievable!"

Bob then composed himself and finished the rest of the meeting. As the staff filed out of the room, he grabbed Tony.

"You sure everything is all right?" he asked in a much-calmer tone.

"No," Tony said. "It's not all right. It's too much to talk about now. But I'll be fine."

Tony grabbed an energy drink from the vending machine. When he got to his desk he slammed down the drink with a handful of ibuprofen, hoping his headache would at least let up.

He heard his phone's text message alert. It was from Andy. "How did it go, my friend?"

Tony answered back, "It didn't. She wasn't home when I got up. Dinner isn't going to be fun tonight."

"Good luck, bro."

Tony checked. Nothing from Katherine and nothing from Angelique. She must be giving him some space which was good because despite what she said about willing to be patient and supportive, he didn't want to have to explain why it wasn't done yet.

He put his phone away in his desk, hoping he could pull it together in time. He was going to quit or be fired very soon, but he was hoping to leave on a high note. He already knew tonight there would be no high notes, and was just looking to survive until 7 p.m.

That afternoon, twins Timmy and Tommy Mitchell were playing football in their backyard. It was only early January, but in the Mitchell backyard, it was already time for the Super Bowl. The Cowboys had never lost a game at Mitchell Stadium, and they already had a big lead in this game.

Cheryl Mitchell was worried about her seven-year-old twins running around outside. She thought it was too cold, but the boys had too much energy. They were too excited about the real Cowboys being in the playoffs. There was another big winter storm on its way this weekend so this was their last chance to play outside for a while. After initially saying no, the boys begging eventually wore her down and she relented as long as they dressed warmly, wore their Cowboys beanies and gloves.

Neither boy could throw well with gloves on, and when Tommy tried to hit Timmy on a deep post pattern, the ball sailed well over his head, over the fence and into the neighbors' yard.

The boys had come up with a special rule for playing in the backyard. When the ball went over the fence into the Jensen yard, the one who threw the ball had to go get it and deal with the mean old man and his big, ugly dog. But went the ball went over the fence into the Michaels yard, the one who threw it had to stay where he was while the other got to go next door to see Mrs. Michaels.

Both of the boys had a crush on the beautiful Mrs. Michaels. She was so sweet to them. Most of the time, Mrs. Michaels would help them get the ball, and she often sent them home with some cookies. This time Timmy was the lucky one.

He sprinted out the side gate to the Michaels front door and rang the bell. There was no answer. Of all the rotten luck, no Mrs. Michaels and no cookies. He headed to their gate and went into the backyard. The ball was easy to find. Timmy tossed it over the fence and started to head home.

Suddenly the silence of the cold gray afternoon was shattered by screams. Cheryl Mitchell raced to the backyard. She only saw Tommy.

"Where's Timmy?" she asked frantically. Tommy pointed toward the Michaels house. Now outside she could tell the screaming was definitely coming from next door.

"Stay here and go inside," Mrs. Mitchell yelled to Tommy as she raced next door to check on her child. She couldn't imagine what would make Timmy scream. The Michaels were always so nice, and they had no animals that might have scared him.

She saw Timmy standing in the middle of the yard. The screams were finished, and he was crying uncontrollably. She raced toward him and picked him up in her arms.

"What's wrong, baby?" she asked Timmy who couldn't speak. But he pointed directly behind his mother.

Mrs. Mitchell turned quickly. Her first frightened glance was too quick and revealed nothing unusual. But as she slowed down and scanned the yard again she screamed herself. She thought she might faint, but she had to get her son out of this yard immediately.

"Close your eyes, baby," Mrs. Mitchell told Timmy. "Just close your eyes. Forget what you saw. Just think about puppies and rainbows."

She hurried home. She covered both boys in blankets and called 911 but was too frightened to speak properly. The 911 operator dispatched the police and paramedics to the Mitchell house and tried to calm the caller down.

"Ma'am, are you okay?"

"No. No. No."

"Ma'am, are you in immediate danger?"

"They're d-d-d-dead."

"Who is dead, ma'am?"

"N-n-next door."

The police arrived and checked on the Mitchell family first. Cheryl Mitchell was still too shaken up to speak well, but she managed to get out enough to let the police know to look in the backyard next door.

The first officer threw up when he saw the head of Katherine Michaels, and then the dismembered bodies of Katherine and young TJ Michaels stacked neatly with the firewood along the side of the house. The second officer called it in.

The CSI unit was already processing the house by the time Detective Frederick Thomas arrived on the scene. He was pointed to the backyard where the coroner was taking pieces of the bodies from the stack of firewood and laying them out like she was putting together a pair of morbid puzzles.

"You have anything for me yet?" Detective Thomas asked.

"Well, factoring in outside weather conditions, liver temp puts the death about three this morning," said Coroner Long. "The bodies are dismembered at the joints. Looks like some kind of power tool. Tough to determine COD right now, but at least some of the cuts were antemortem. And Mrs. Thomas was pregnant. I'm guessing five to six months."

"Anything else?" asked Thomas.

"Yeah, take a look at these cuts," said Long, handing Katherine's right forearm to the detective. "Whoever did this cauterized the wounds to limit the blood loss after each cut."

"We're dealing with one sadistic son of a bitch here," stated Thomas.

"It definitely looks that way," said Long. "If it's all right with you, I would like to take the bodies back to the lab now. I'll call you if I find anything."

"Yeah, get out of here," said Thomas. "I'm going to check out the house."

Thomas met CSI Lopez in the house who filled him in.

"The house is clean, and I mean SPOTLESS except for the fireplace," Lopez informed Thomas. "Come take a look."

Lopez led him into the living room. Thomas noted that a house like this probably used a professional cleaning service. He needed to find out who serviced the house and the date of the last service.

In the fireplace there were mostly ashes, but there was a partially burned gray Northwestern football sweatshirt with blood spatter.

"That's good," said Thomas. "What else?"

"You need to check out the garage," Lopez said, leading Thomas in that direction.

"We found blood on only one saw and just the blade," Lopez said. "The rest of the saw is clean. The killer must have been in a rush, wiped it all down but forgot the blade. Doesn't smell like cleaning products. I think whoever did this may have taken the blood with him."

"One sick motherfucker for sure," Thomas said matter-of-factly. "Gonna be fun taking him down."

"One more unusual thing about the garage," continued Lopez. "We dusted everything in this garage and couldn't find a single print anywhere. Not on the tools, the toolbox, the workbench, the doors. They all look well used. Somebody took the time to wipe down everything, even her car."

"That is unusual," Thomas said. "What about the house? Any prints? Forced entry? Anything else?"

"No signs of forced entry anywhere so the perp must have known the victims," Lopez replied. "Only prints so far match either the victims or the husband."

"Well, that makes sense," said Thomas. "The first suspect in these cases is always the husband. And where is Mr. Michaels at the moment?"

"You're kidding, right?" asked Lopez.

"Look at me, Lopez," Thomas said. "Am I EVER kidding?"

"No, sorry," Lopez answered. "I just figured you knew. Tony Michaels. He's on billboards everywhere. He should be on the air right now."

"I don't need any 'should be' right now," Thomas said forcefully. "Because if he isn't, he could be long gone."

Thomas grabbed the remote, turned on the TV and changed to Channel 9. Sure enough, there was Tony Michaels, "The Most Trusted Man in Texas," anchoring the news.

"Motherfucker!" Thomas shouted, then regrouped.

"Okay, we have two options," he said turning toward CSI Lopez. "One—this is one sick bastard, and he's so cocky that he thinks he can go to work and get away with this. Maybe he planned to burn the bodies but didn't have enough time after all the cleanup. He went to work figuring the bodies wouldn't be found, intending to dispose of them and destroy any evidence remaining when he gets home tonight."

"What's the other option?" Lopez asked.

"Well, the other option isn't very likely," Thomas paused. "But the only other possibility is that this poor bastard somehow went to work with no idea where his wife and son were. It's hard to imagine that being the case, but that's the only way he could be on the air right now if he's human.

"I need your team to keep going over this house," Thomas continued. "If our newsboy is the killer, we need to make sure he gets the needle for killing his pregnant wife and little boy. If he is innocent, which I am sure he will claim, then there has to be something to back him up."

"We'll keep looking, Detective," Lopez said confidently. "If there's anything here, my team will find it."

"Good," said Thomas. "One more thing."

"What's that?" asked Lopez.

"I'm assuming y'all took pictures of the bodies while they were still stacked up, before Doc Long moved them?"

"Of course," Lopez replied. "She wouldn't have touched the bodies if we didn't."

"How soon can you get me prints of those photos?" Thomas asked.

"I have a printer in the back of my car," Lopez said with a smile.

"My man!" shouted Thomas. "Let's take a walk. I'll get me some pictures, then I'll take a couple of boys down to Channel

9 and have a little talk with this newsboy of ours. I wonder if I make it on TV. I sure hope they get my good side."

Lopez just laughed. Soon, he handed the photos to Thomas and walked back in the house.

Detective Thomas and two uniformed police officers arrived at Channel 9, just as the news broadcast was wrapping up. News director Bob Dunham went subtly searching for cameramen. He told three of them to follow the officers as discreetly as possible from different angles. Maybe it was nothing, but if there was going to be anything newsworthy happening in his newsroom, he was going to get it on film.

Dunham then went to greet Detective Thomas and the two officers.

"We're here to speak to Tony Michaels," Thomas said politely.

"Sure," Bob said. "I'll take you to his desk. Is he in trouble?"

"We just need to talk to him," Thomas said calmly. "We should be in and out."

While walking to Tony's desk Thomas received a text from CSI Lopez. "Found Michaels's Rose Bowl ring with blood on it." The picture was attached.

Thomas approached Michaels and introduced himself. The two officers stood silently behind him.

"Mr. Michaels," Thomas started, "where were you last night?"

"I went to Hooters last night," Tony responded. "Then went straight home. Why?"

"We'll get to that," Thomas said. "We're just having a conversation here. Just relax and be honest with me and we can go on with our business. Now, what time did you get home from Hooters?"

"Not sure exactly, but it was somewhere between midnight and 12:30."

"Did you get into any kind of argument with your wife?"

"No, she was asleep when I got home."

"Did you stay up, play video games, watch a movie or anything?"

"Honestly, I drank too much. I went upstairs, threw up and passed out on the floor."

"Did you hear anything in the middle of the night? Any strange noises? Did you see anything?"

"I have no idea where you're going with this, but I don't remember anything from the time I was on the floor until the time I woke up," Tony said, starting to panic.

Thomas gestured toward Tony to stay calm, then continued. "Did you leave the house at any point in the night? Have anyone over? Anything at all out of the ordinary?"

"Like I said, I came home, passed out and that was it."

"So you were home at around 3 a.m. then?"

"Yeah."

"Sleeping?"

"Yes."

"I find that very interesting, Mr. Michaels. You were home alone with your family at 3 a.m. and nothing unusual happened."

"Yep."

"Well, Mr. Michaels, please stay calm. I hate to be the one to tell you this, but your wife and child are dead. I'm very sorry for your loss. Now what I would like is for you to calmly get up and go for a ride with us to the station. We can get your statement and we'll get to the bottom of this."

"What the fuck is going on here?" Michaels shouted as he stood. "This isn't happening. You want me to go to the station? This can't be real. You can't think I did this?"

Thomas remained cool. He gestured again for Tony to stay calm.

"Nobody has accused anybody of anything just yet. But we do have some questions. And you were at the scene of the crime. We just need to talk to you, rule you out as a suspect. I assumed you would rather do that in private down at the station than here in front of your coworkers and I don't see them right now, but I assume we have some cameras on us."

"This is fucking ridiculous!" Tony shouted, his face was somewhere between Northwestern purple and Ohio State scarlet. Tony was confused and disoriented. His head was throbbing, and there were tears streaming down his cheeks. "What the fuck is happening?"

"Now, Mr. Michaels," Thomas said. He was still relaxed but his voice was growing sterner. "I have been asking you nicely to stay calm. I don't want these two fellas behind me here to have to do anything except stand behind me and watch, but you're making that more difficult. I suggest you have a sip of that water there and have a seat."

Michaels grabbed his water bottle from his desk and took a few sips, but he didn't sit down.

Thomas pulled his phone out of his pocket and showed the picture of Tony's Rose Bowl ring.

"Now, Mr. Michaels, is this your ring?"

"Yes."

"Yeah, that was one hell of a game you played," Thomas smiled. "You had a cannon for an arm. I can still remember all those touchdowns you threw. Won me some money betting on you too. Damn shame about that arm injury, you could have been special. A lot of teams could use a quarterback like we saw in that game. Damn shame."

Thomas shook his head. Michaels was still standing, dizzied by everything that was happening around him. He wasn't even sure where he was.

"You know what else is a damn shame?" Thomas asked but didn't pause long enough for a reply. "Your wife's blood is on that ring. And it's also on your sweatshirt that you didn't do a very good job of burning. Your little boy's blood is on that sweatshirt too."

"Fuck you. Go to hell."

Thomas had run out of patience. He grabbed the photos of the bodies stacked in the woodpile and threw them on the desk in front of Tony.

"Are you proud of this? Because this is going to be your legacy. 'Most Trusted Man in Texas,' my ass!" Thomas laughed. He looked at the officers, then nodded his head in Tony's direction.

"Cuff him, boys. Mr. Michaels, you are under arrest."

One of the officers approached Tony and grabbed his arm. Overwhelmed by the situation, Tony instinctively punched the officer in his jaw, knocking him over the neighboring desk. The second officer hit Tony with pepper spray to subdue him, got him to the ground and cuffed him.

"We could have done this the easy way," Thomas chastised. "I would advise you to learn some manners quickly unless you really want that needle. These gentlemen will read you your rights on the way out."

There wasn't a sound in the entire Channel 9 building as Thomas led his officers and Tony out of the building. There was no movement except for the one cameraman who followed the foursome to the exit.

Finally, Bob Dunham's voice shattered the silence. "Holy shit! That was amazing," Bob shouted victoriously. "Please tell me you guys got film of that!"

There were a few gasps of horror at Bob's celebratory tone.

"Now listen up, everybody," he shouted. "I do not give a DAMN what you think of Tony. I don't care if he was your best friend. THIS is fucking news! We have exclusive footage, and we are the first to know about this. It is our job to report this, and we WILL report this. We will dig out every detail we can.

"This footage is going to make this station a lot of money when we sell it to the networks tomorrow," he said. "But first, we're going to get ahead of this. I need everybody to be ready to go on the air in ten minutes. We are going to cut in on whatever is on the air with breaking news. We are going to show our footage repeatedly.

"I want a crew at his house by the time we get on the air. This is our ONLY story right now and we are going to dominate covering it. Nobody will beat us to any detail of this story. We need to be the only source for people on this story. If you get beat to something, you are fired. And if you're not on board with this, you're fired! Now get your asses ready to go!"

Tony's regular coanchor Tracy Justice had left a few minutes before the broadcast ended to attend her son's basketball game and just missed out on all the commotion. The regular 10 o'clock anchors hadn't gone to makeup yet. Young gorgeous

Lynne Bozeman, the reporter Dunham hired to try to replace some of the sizzle Channel 9 lost when Angelique quit, saw this as her big break and volunteered to take the lead on the story.

"Fine," Dunham said. "This is your big shot. Make it count."

Bob Dunham hustled into his office to make calls to let the suits know they would be breaking in with live coverage. He would wait to call the networks until after Channel 9 had it on the air. He didn't want to tip anybody off. He wanted other stations to find out from his station. He was eager to see how much they would pay for rights to his exclusive footage. This one night was going to make his career. He may have lost his best anchor, but this would give Channel 9 more than enough momentum to make up for that.

At the police station, the officers led Tony to the booking area with instructions to take him to an interrogation room as soon as he was booked. Detective Thomas headed to autopsy.

"Any good news for me, Doc?" Thomas asked.

"I'm not sure," responded Dr. Long. "I did notice one thing I didn't see at the scene."

"What's that, Doc?"

"There is a small stab wound through Mrs. Michaels' navel. Could be a steak knife or other small weapon. Whatever the weapon was, it pierced the fetus and killed the baby.

"It was likely the first wound she suffered and was definitely prior to her death," Dr. Long continued. "Perhaps it was done to torture her psychologically. Her assailant wanted her to suffer the loss of the baby before he did any real damage to her."

"Okay," Thomas interrupted, "tell me about how she was cut up."

"Well, she was dismembered in thirteen different places, including the decapitation. Seven of the wounds are antemortem: Both ankles, both knees, the left wrist, elbow and shoulder. All of the wounds were cauterized so the assailant was sealing the wounds up as he cut. Her COD was actually a massive heart attack, due to the all the trauma. The rest of the cuts, including the beheading, were after she was dead."

"Anything else about the mother?" Thomas inquired.

"It's strange," Dr. Long answered, "but there isn't a single defensive wound on her body. There's no sign of trauma to her head. No ligature marks to suggest she was bound at any time. No bruising. No tissue under her fingernails. No signs of struggle anywhere."

"Your point, Doc?"

"Well, if all of the cuts were postmortem, based on the wound to the abdomen, I might have thought it was a suicide attempt. The angle of the wound suggests it could be self-inflicted. Perhaps the marriage was in trouble. The husband came home, saw her lying on the floor and instead of calling 911, he panicked and decided to get rid of the evidence to cover up the suicide."

"Not a smart plan, but somewhat plausible," Thomas said.

"I would agree with you, Detective," Dr. Long answered. "But only if the dismemberment were all postmortem. Whoever cut her up started to do so while she was alive. But the cuts are too even, and again, no signs that despite being a perfectly healthy, physically fit young woman, she made any effort to stop what was happening."

"That makes no sense," Thomas said. "Unless she was drugged. Maybe chloroform or roofies or something like that."

"I've already sent a sample of her blood for a tox screen," Dr. Long said. "Maybe they'll have an answer for us."

"Thanks, Doc," Thomas said. "What about the boy?"

"The boy is a little different, but close," Dr. Long said. "All of the cuts were made antemortem and the wounds were not cauterized until postmortem. The boy bled out. Perhaps the killer was showing the boy some mercy and let him die quickly, while the wife had to suffer. Also, there was no attempt to decapitate the boy."

"Thanks, Doc. Great work!"

The lab results on Katherine's blood were not ready yet, so Detective Thomas headed to interrogation. He found Tony Michaels sobbing with his head in his arms on the interrogation table. As Thomas walked in, a nearly lifeless Tony sat up. This was not the same Tony Michaels the public was used to seeing on the Channel 9 news, and it wasn't the same Tony Michaels who had punched a police officer earlier that evening.

At Channel 9, Tony's first reaction had been shock and anger. That mixed with the lingering hangover had made it impossible to process the situation. Now that he had some time to sit quietly, it hit him that Katherine and TJ were dead. The sadness was overwhelming.

"Now, Mr. Michaels," Thomas said quietly, "I hope that your behavior will be better than it was earlier today. That kind of thing only makes matters worse for you, you understand?"

Tony nodded. He didn't even remember punching the

officer. He had nothing to hide, and he felt like he needed to do some damage control, so he agreed to talk without a lawyer present, until he felt it necessary.

"Good. Now may I offer you a beverage?" Thomas asked. "Coffee? Water?"

"No, thanks," said Tony, shaking his head slowly.

"Okay, if you change your mind, let me know," Thomas said, still speaking in a soft voice. "May I call you Tony?"

Again, Tony nodded.

"Now, Tony, here's my dilemma," Thomas said. "I have a house where two dead bodies were found. There are no signs of forced entry, and my best forensics team can't find any evidence that anybody besides you and the two victims were ever in that house. Their blood is on the ring you admitted to wearing last night. Their blood is on the sweatshirt you were wearing last night at Hooters, which we know because your buddy Andy posted a picture on Twitter.

"You admit to being home at the time of the murders, and your sweatshirt was partially burned in your fireplace, suggesting you were trying to destroy evidence. Your boss told me you got to work late, looking disheveled and stressed. But you claim you didn't do it. Can you explain that?"

"I can't," said Tony tearfully. "I didn't do it, though. There's no way I would hurt Katherine or TJ. I've been going through a lot lately, so I went to Hooters last night to blow off some steam. I had way too much to drink. I should have never driven home, but I did. Somehow I made it. They were both in their beds when I got home. I passed out on the floor. I woke up in bed without my clothes on. I usually sleep naked. I figured Katherine woke up, saw me, helped me get undressed and get in bed. When I woke up it was already afternoon. I figured they just left so the house would be quiet for me to sleep it off."

"So nothing seemed at all unusual to you?" Thomas asked.

"Honestly," Tony answered, "I woke up too late to really notice anything. Katherine often takes TJ on play dates or to the mall, so it wasn't unusual for them to be gone. I had a terrible hangover. I felt like shit, and it was late. I was in a rush to get to work, so if there was anything, I probably wouldn't have noticed."

"Tony, you said you had a lot going on," said Thomas. "Please fill me in. Were you and the wife having problems?"

"I've been cheating on Katherine," Tony admitted as the tears started back up. "I was planning on asking her for a divorce."

"So you asked, she said no. You guys fought, and somewhere things got a little out of control?" asked Thomas.

"No, it's not like that at all," Tony said. "Everything I have told you is the truth. She was asleep when I got home and not there when I woke up. I can't explain any of this. I haven't been in love with Katherine for a long time, but she was a wonderful person and a great mother. I wanted out of the marriage, but I was happy to give her the house and whatever money I had to give her. She deserved somebody better than me. She didn't deserve to die."

"Now, Tony," said Thomas, "in Texas, we do have the death penalty, and we do use that. We have enough evidence to convict you for three murders, including your unborn daughter. Personally, when I see crimes like this I think lethal injection is far too nice a way to go. But unfortunately, that is currently the only method allowed in this state. I am going to see to it that whoever killed your family gets the needle. If it's you, I will volunteer myself. You understand?"

Tony nodded.

"If you have anything else you want to confess to me right now, it might help you later on, and if you want any hope of not seeing me smiling as I give you the needle, this might be your best shot," Thomas said.

"I've told you everything I know," said Tony.

"Just for fun," Thomas said, "I am going to acknowledge for a moment the possibility that you are telling me the truth. Who could hate you or Katherine enough to do this? You saw the pictures. This wasn't an accident. This was brutal. And it was personal. If, in the unlikely event you are telling the truth, you need to help me out here and tell me who could have done this and set you up. Otherwise, you are probably going to die for this, based on the evidence."

Tony thought momentarily. He thought Angelique had enough passion and fire to kill Katherine if she had to get her out of the way. But he could only imagine something quick and simple like a gunshot, possibly a stabbing or maybe a blow to the head. She definitely wasn't capable of anything like he saw in the pictures. Plus, the timing made no sense. Now that he had promised Angelique he was getting a divorce, Tony was sure Angelique would have been patient. She could have killed Katherine only if Tony let it drag out too long. Angelique had never hidden any of her true feelings with him.

Tony thought if Angelique had ever even thought about

killing Katherine, she would have been bold enough to tell him in some way. And there was no way Angelique would have harmed TJ. It definitely wasn't Angelique.

"I wish I could answer that question, Detective," Tony said. "I really do."

"Well, you need to get yourself a good lawyer," Thomas said. "Maybe your lawyer can help you figure this out. We'll keep searching for evidence, and maybe we'll find something new. But in the meantime, we are charging you with three counts of capital murder. You will be held in jail overnight and see the judge in the morning.

"If the judge sets a bail and you can post it, then you are free as long as you follow all the rules they tell you," Thomas continued. "You won't be able to go home until it's cleared, but maybe find yourself a nice hotel in town for a while and clear your head. If the judge denies bail, then good luck on the inside. Do you understand me?"

Tony nodded. Thomas motioned for the officers outside to come in and take Tony to jail.

Tony made a phone call was to Jake Wood, an attorney who had been the unofficial lawyer of the Dallas Cowboys during Tony's brief stint working out with the team. Any time a player ran into any sort of trouble, Jake Wood was called. The charges were usually dropped quietly or reduced to something insignificant. Tony didn't know who else to call, but if Jake Wood took his case, he thought it would be his best chance. Wood agreed to take the case.

After his phone call, Tony was processed and his personal belongings gathered. As he was being led to his cell, a few of the inmates recognized him.

"Well, well, well," he heard a voice shout. "We got ourselves a celebrity."

"Hey, Mr. Newsman," shouted another voice. "How's this for news? Our top story tonight is you sucking my dick. How you like that?"

There were a few other taunts, but Tony never looked up or acknowledged them in any way. He went quietly to his cell and cried himself to sleep.

After Tony was taken away by the officers, Thomas left the interrogation room, shaking his head. Lou Ruggles, the Dallas chief of police, greeted him immediately.

"Well?" said Ruggles. "Fill me in. I already have every media outlet in the country on my ass over this."

"We have enough physical evidence for a conviction," Thomas said. "But something doesn't add up."

"If we have enough to convict him, then what exactly is the problem?" Ruggles asked.

"I don't know, sir," Thomas said. "I talked to the coroner and some things I saw at the scene just didn't seem right. Plus, if he is guilty, he is the best liar I have ever seen. I mean, he has no alibi, but he's pretty convincing. Unless we find something new, he's our guy though."

"Then he's our guy," Ruggles said emphatically. "Don't doubt yourself, Detective. Just make sure he doesn't walk on this. And don't make any mistakes. By morning it will look like Dallas is hosting a worldwide news convention."

Tony spent the night in his cell, crying as quietly as he could. There were plenty of heckles and threats, but no incidents. Sleep was difficult to come by as his mind was racing. It was hard to believe this was real, but it was. Tony struggled to figure out who could have done such a terrible thing and why. He was also beating himself up for allowing it to happen. How had he not been awakened at some point? Surely Katherine was screaming, and he slept through it.

When sleep did come, there were nightmares. In the nightmares, Tony watched in horror as a faceless man murdered his wife and child. Katherine would call out to Tony for help, but Tony could do nothing but watch helplessly. Though the man was faceless, Tony could definitely see a smile. The man was enjoying it. He could see the man cutting Katherine into pieces on the saw he bought to build TJ's crib. The more Katherine screamed, the more paralyzed Tony became. When the screaming stopped, the man grabbed Katherine's dismembered hand, turned toward Tony and waved her hand with that creepy faceless smile.

Tony would wake, drenched in sweat, shivering with fear. He contemplated suicide, searching the cell for anything he could use, but decided that would just make him look guilty, and it wouldn't help anything. He had to make sure Angelique knew he didn't do this. He tried to think about how happy he had been just a day before. He tried to imagine the joy and the love he felt in that last shower with her. But now the faceless smile followed his consciousness wherever he tried to take it. There was no escape.

In the morning, Tony met briefly with his attorney at the jail before appearing in front of the judge. Tony appeared weak, fragile and helpless. He hadn't stopped crying since he was led away from Channel 9. The district attorney argued that with the heinous nature of the crime, Tony should be held without bail. Wood made an impassioned plea that his client was innocent and clearly distraught by the loss of his family. In his current state, Tony posed no flight risk and no danger to others.

Wood further argued that if held in prison, Tony was a suicide risk and the best way to ensure that he made it to trial, thereby assuring the facts of the case were presented in court, was to grant bail. The judge reluctantly agreed, setting bail at $5 million on the stipulation that Tony seek regular psychiatric treatment while free. If he missed any appointments or attempted to harm himself, bail would be revoked.

Tony had done quite well investing what was left of the insurance money from his arm injury after purchasing the house and Katherine's ring. The couple had lived well within their means with a comfortable but simple life and with no house payment, it was easy to save money on Tony's salary. Tony had enough to post bail.

Tony collected his personal belongings and left with Wood to go to his office. On the drive, Wood told Tony that his office would set him up in a hotel room. He wouldn't be able to go home because the crime scene had not yet been cleared, but he probably didn't want to go there anyway with all the news vans camped out on his street. Wood suggested that Tony stay at the hotel, even after the house was cleared, just to stay out of the spotlight. Wood said he would send somebody to Tony's house to gather whatever he needed once the house was cleared. Wood asked if Tony needed anything in the meantime.

"A phone charger," Tony said. "And something for my headache."

"I can get you both of those back at my office," Wood said. "Anything else?"

"Just answers."

Wood brought Tony into his office and invited him to sit down. Wood's secretary brought in a bottle of water and some ibuprofen.

"Okay," Wood said, handing Tony a spare phone charger from the top drawer of his desk, "you need to tell me everything you know, and I mean, everything. No matter how insignificant you might think it is, I need to know. We'll get the photos from the house, and I need you to tell me if ANYTHING seems wrong in any of the rooms."

Tony nodded as Wood continued.

"Before we start, though, you should realize a few things: One, the video of you punching that cop has been on the air nonstop, the photo pulled from that video is on the front page of every newspaper. Now when it gets to court, I'm confident I can get that killed and not allowed in the trial, but it will be hard to find jurors who haven't seen that, and even though the judge will instruct them otherwise, they will likely be biased by that in some way.

"Second, the nature of the killings is going to bring out the worst in all of your media cohorts. You need to lay as low as possible until, as well as during, the trial. Let me do all of your talking for you. Go nowhere except court, my office and your psych appointments, which I will try to arrange at my office.

"Third, you hired me, and I accepted this case. There is nothing I hate more than losing. But based on what we know right now, it doesn't look good. I am going to do everything earthly possible to find anything that will put doubt in the mind of the jurors. If the police made any mistakes, I will be all over it to help take the focus off of you.

"The problem here is you have no alibi," Wood continued as Tony sipped his water and listened. "Now, I checked at Hooters, and I saw your bar tab. Based on how many drinks you had, your blood alcohol level was well over the legal limit at the time of the murders. I have no idea how you made it home that night. I can't imagine you could have pulled this off in your state. The cuts were clean and you have no wounds, and I don't think you could have cleaned up in time. It may turn out to be a really good thing you were that drunk. But until we find something else to hang our hat on, that defense is pretty weak. I need anything from you that might help."

Tony nodded in agreement, and then told Jake everything: the New York job, their fight over it, Tony's first infidelity, everything that had happened with Angelique, the Los Angeles job and his decision to ask for a divorce.

"Did you talk to her about a divorce?" Wood asked.

"I never had the chance," Tony responded. "I didn't decide on it for sure until Wednesday. I was planning on telling her Thursday, but she wasn't home. I love Katherine, but I was no longer in love with her. We just weren't right for each other."

"Okay," Wood began again. "You are a fairly wealthy man and I'm guessing a divorce would have cost you at least a couple of million dollars. The prosecution will use that as motive. They will also use her holding you back in your career as motive. They have seen the video of you punching a police officer and will portray you as a shitty individual. They will make you out to be a violent, ill-tempered, alcoholic liar. When they do, I don't want you to react in any way.

"When the time comes, I will go over how I want you to behave in court," Wood went on. "But for now, they are going to paint a really ugly picture of you in the media. It is important that you do not give them anything else to feed on. They are already circling like vultures. Don't trust any of them. Don't read anything written about you, and for God's sake, don't watch any news. I don't care if they are talking about the Middle East—*don't* watch it.

"As far as your girlfriend goes," Wood said, "it's best if you avoid her. If you get caught with her, it's only going to make you look worse. I mean no offense, but no matter how pure your love may be, they will turn it into something ugly. And if you're banging some hot piece of ass while on trial for murdering your wife, that's going to look *really* bad on your part. They will be just as brutal on her as they are on you. They might try to make her out to be an uglier person than you, maybe even try to say this was her idea. So it's best for BOTH of you to avoid each other. And don't forget, she is still part of the media."

"I need her to know that I didn't do this," Tony said. "I need her to know that I love her. And I need her."

"Let me talk to her," Wood said. He waved in his secretary. "Miss Cook is going to take you to your hotel. You are already checked in, just go straight to your room, clean up, order room service and get as much rest as you can. Anything you need, you contact me. If you can't reach me, contact Miss Cook. Now, I need to get to work saving your butt."

Miss Cook drove Tony to the hotel and brought him straight to the room. Along the route between the office and the hotel, Tony noticed a crew replacing one of his billboards. By that afternoon every billboard bearing Tony's likeness has been replaced by either a generic Channel 9 ad or one for the billboard company itself. They were not wasting any time distancing themselves from him.

At the hotel, Miss Cook gave him all the information he needed to contact her or Jake Wood. Before leaving she asked his shirt, pant and shoe size.

Tony took a long, hot shower, then took a nap. He woke to a knock at the door. It was Miss Cook. She returned with shopping bags full of clothes as well as some toiletries.

"I tried to guess your style," she said. "I hope I wasn't too far off, but this should be enough clothes to last until you are able to go to your house. And I bought some running shoes in case you want to use the hotel gym."

"Thank you," Tony said, relieved to have something else to wear.

"I tried calling you," Miss Cook said. "But it went straight to voice mail. You should really keep your phone on in case Mr. Wood needs to reach you."

"Oh crap," Tony said, mad at himself for forgetting to charge his phone. He plugged it in and promised it would not happen again.

"I am sure Mr. Wood told you," said Miss Cook, "but the police will likely be monitoring your phone so be mindful of that with any calls, texts or e-mails. As much as possible, I would advise you to avoid the Internet and all social media. It's pretty ugly right now."

Tony nodded.

"Have they come up with a nickname for me yet?" he asked.

"They are calling you The Anchor of Death," Miss Cook said in an apologetic tone.

"Can you believe this?" Tony asked. "This was the career I always dreamed of, and they've already convicted me and reduced me to a bad pun."

"I'm so sorry," Miss Cook said. "As per the judge's order, Mr. Wood has set up your first psychiatric appointment. It will be Thursday of next week in a small conference room at our office. I will come pick you up. Until then, get as much rest as you can, call if you need anything and try to stay positive."

"Jake is very good," Miss Cook said, using the attorney's first name for the first time. It sounded strange to Tony's ear as she had been so formal to that point. He didn't even know Miss Cook's first name. Now was probably not the time to ask. "He will do everything he can for you."

With that, Miss Cook left the room. Tony checked his phone. There were several voice mails and texts. He immediately deleted any message from a number he didn't recognize or those he recognized as reporters.

There were a few supportive texts from Andy and several texts from Angelique, many begging Tony to call her. The final one simply said, "I love you."

Tony replied, "My lawyer thinks we shouldn't talk. But I love you, and I miss you."

The phone rang immediately. Tony contemplated letting it go to voice mail but knew he couldn't. Tony didn't have many friends left. He couldn't afford to lose Angelique now.

"I don't care what the lawyer says," Angelique started shouting before Tony could even say hello. "I need you. I need to know you're okay. And you need somebody by your side."

"Sweetie, you have to listen," Tony said. "You know I need you so much right now and holding you would make everything feel better, but understand how it will look right now. And if anybody finds out about us, they will treat you just as badly as they treat me."

"Tony, I quit my job," Angelique said, causing Tony to sit down in shock. "You know I go to bed early because of the job, so I didn't know anything that had happened. We were doing the show and we were told to cut to a live shot for breaking news. I didn't know, but it was a reporter on your front lawn accusing you of this. Then we showed footage of you hitting that cop. I lost it and walked off the set."

"Baby, I'm sorry," Tony said mainly because he didn't have any idea what to say.

"Since then, I have just been crying, and all I've eaten is ice cream," Angelique told him. "I'm probably really gross right now, but I need to see you. I need you to hold me and tell me you didn't do this and that everything will be okay. And then I want you to promise me that when this is all over, we'll move far away from Dallas."

"I know this is difficult," Tony said, "but I need you to be strong right now. You've always been the strong one. I need that Angelique. You know I wouldn't have hurt Katherine and especially TJ. You also know I wouldn't have done anything to jeopardize our future together.

"Right now," Tony continued, "I need you to call my lawyer. At some point the police will probably want to talk to you. They might even accuse you of putting me up to this and threaten you with bullshit conspiracy charges. If they do, just do whatever my lawyer advises you to do. Call him before you do anything else. And we can't talk or see each other until he says it's okay."

"I love you so much, Tony," Angelique whimpered, her voice shaking as she tried to regroup enough for the lioness to take over.

"I love you too, Angelique," Tony said. "I miss you."

Detective Thomas went back to the Michaels house looking for more answers. There should have been so much more blood everywhere—in the garage, in the kitchen, in the carpet by the fireplace, and even though the wounds were cauterized, maybe some along the side of the house by the firewood.

If Tony Michaels had taken the time to clean up so well and burn whatever else was burned in the fire, why had he been careless enough to leave his sweatshirt half-burnt? True, Tony probably wasn't counting on anybody finding the bodies so quickly. He could have taken a break to go to work to act like nothing was unusual, and then go back home and finish disposing of the evidence or even skip town.

If he had cleaned up so well, why weren't there signs of any unusual cleaning or any chemical odor? Detective Thomas had been at more than a few crime scenes reeking of bleach or other cleaning products. And why put the bodies outside in the first place? If it wasn't for the neighbor boys playing football, they wouldn't have been discovered. But why take that risk? If they had just been left in the garage or anywhere in the house, the bodies would never have been found. Tony would have been able to continue to do whatever he had planned next.

"Quit asking so many questions," Thomas told himself. He remembered what Chief Ruggles told him earlier. There was more than enough evidence to convict him. But his gut told him to keep asking questions.

Thomas called CSI Lopez. "Did we get the tox results back on Mrs. Michaels yet?" he asked.

"We did, but it's no help," Lopez said. "She had no alcohol, no drugs and no known chemicals in her system. We got a warrant to check the trash of all his neighbors and Channel 9, found nothing at all."

"What about the car?" Thomas asked. "Did we get anything there?"

"Another goose egg," Lopez replied. "The car definitely hasn't been detailed in a while, but as far as this case, it's really clean."

"He admitted to cheating on his wife," Thomas said. "Did we check at his girlfriend's place? Maybe she helped him out or let him hide stuff there."

"Send me her info and I'll get a warrant and go check it out," said Lopez. "I'll bring somebody with me to share in the fun of dumpster diving."

Angelique's apartment was searched and other than it being a bit of a mess, nothing was unusual. Tony kept a few clothes in her apartment, but there was nothing to suggest he had gone by her apartment after the murders. The dumpsters came up empty as well. The police took Angelique's journal, laptop and phone but found nothing to suggest any plot between the two, nor contact between the two between the time of the murder and Tony's arrest.

Angelique was brought in for questioning, so she called Jake Wood who met her at the station and calmed her down.

"They don't have anything to suggest you have any involvement," Wood told her. "If they try to get a rise out of you, just keep your cool. I will step in when needed. You'll be fine, and hopefully, we're in and out."

"Thanks."

Detective Thomas entered the interrogation room and immediately got under Angelique's skin.

"So, you like sleeping with married men, breaking up families?"

Wood could see the fire rising in Angelique and spoke up before she could get a word out. "Adultery isn't against the law, Detective," Wood said. "My client was in a loving relationship."

"Adultery may not be against the law," Thomas replied, "but it does speak to character. And the man in this supposed loving relationship was married to somebody else, who was brutally and sadistically murdered. With the wife out of the picture, that makes things easier for you, doesn't it?"

"Just because I fucked a married man doesn't mean I would do any harm to his wife," Angelique answered. "And just because Tony was fucking a woman who wasn't his wife doesn't mean he would want to harm his wife. Tony cared about Katherine. He just wasn't in love with her anymore. And please explain how THIS is easier.

"If you think he did this, you're crazy," Angelique continued. "Tony is the sweetest, calmest, most peaceful man I've ever known. I've never seen him get angry, and to be honest, there have been a few times he maybe should have been angry with me. There is no way he did this. You should have seen how he lit up around TJ. Even just talking about his son made him radiant."

"So it didn't bother you that he would go home to another woman?" Thomas prodded.

"Of course it bothered me," Angelique said. "But I knew

the situation from the beginning. Having him part-time was better than any man I've dated full-time. When we were together he was there 100 percent. We were very happy. I wanted more. But I understood. I was willing to be patient. He had just promised me he would ask for a divorce."

"But that divorce would have cost him, and by extension, you, millions of dollars," Thomas said. "Plus, leaving a pregnant wife would make him look pretty bad to lots of folks. His career would have been in trouble."

"Tony didn't care about the money," Angelique replied. "He said he would give her whatever she needed, and we would still have plenty to make a new start. If it wasn't in broadcasting, he could teach or coach football. You can try all you want to fabricate motive, but Tony had none, and neither did I."

The questioning continued for a while. Angelique stayed strong. The lioness wanted to roar, but except for a few snarls, Angelique kept her composure. Wood stepped in occasionally. Thomas eventually accepted that Angelique was not going to give him anything useful. And Angelique was at Channel 6 at the time of the murder so she wasn't a suspect.

"Okay, ma'am," Thomas said, "you are free to go."

In the parking lot, Wood advised Angelique on how to proceed. He gave her as much information as he could about what to expect from the rest of the investigation and eventually the trial.

"I understand you quit your job," Wood asked. "Will you be all right financially? Is there anything I can do to help? Do you need anything?"

"I need you to win this case," Angelique said. "And I need to see Tony."

"I'm afraid that isn't a great idea right now," Wood re-sponded. "If you're seen together it will look bad for everyone."

"I *need* to see him," Angelique pleaded. "I need to know he's okay."

The police released the Michaels house. Jake Wood went to visit Tony at his hotel to let him know.

"You can go home if you want, but I imagine there are still reporters waiting outside with nothing better to do than harass you," Wood said. "If you want to remain here and there are things you need from the house I can get them for you, or send Miss Cook."

"I can't go back to live at that house," Tony said. "There's no way I could sleep knowing what happened. I have enough difficulty here with the nightmares. I'll go with you. We can grab some clothes, and I'll give you a list of everything I want to keep. We can put it in the hotel or store it, maybe some of it at Angelique's.

"Anything that's left give to a charity, if they will take it," Tony continued. "If not, throw it away. I want as few remind-ers as possible of that house. Then see if you can find a realtor who will list the house. I don't know if anybody will want it, but I want to sell it if I can."

"I will get on that," Wood responded. "Do you want to go by the house now or do you need more time? Do you want us to scout it out and wait until there are fewer reporters?"

"Let's get it over with," Tony said.

At the house for the first time since learning of the mur-ders, Tony had a very uneasy feeling. The police had allowed

Jake Wood to have Tony's garage door opener from his car. Wood made his way through a sea of reporters. The three entered the house without saying a word. Tony saw photographs of Katherine and TJ and began to have an anxiety attack. Miss Cook grabbed his hand and tried to calm Tony down.

"If you're not up for this," Wood said, "we can do it another time. Or we can do it by photographs at the hotel or in my office."

"No," Tony said. "I need to do this, and waiting will only make it worse, not better. Let's just try to be quick."

Miss Cook got out her notebook and digital voice recorder and began taking notes as Tony identified the items he wanted to keep. There were a few items Tony skipped that Miss Cook thought might have value and double-checked to be sure Tony didn't want them.

"No," Tony said. "If you like it, feel free to take it for yourself. Otherwise, find a charity or church to take it."

"Some of these items might sell well, Mr. Michaels," said Miss Cook.

"No, I'm not going to sell anything," Tony answered. "It wouldn't be right. If a charity wants to sell stuff, that's fine. But I don't want the money."

They all heard a noise upstairs, the sound of something breaking. Tony sprinted up the stairs, skipping several steps with each stride. In his office he found a reporter taking photographs. The reporter also had a backpack full of items that he was pilfering, possibly as souvenirs, but likely to sell.

Tony let out a barbaric scream. The rage of everything that had happened exploded in that moment. He punched the reporter as hard as he could, breaking his nose and sending blood racing out of the reporter's face. The reporter staggered but remained upright. Tony hit him again, this time breaking his jaw. Three teeth flew through the air, were briefly highlighted by a small sliver of sunlight coming through a crack in the blinds and disappeared into the corner of Tony's bookcase. The reporter fell to the ground and dropped his camera. Tony got on top of the man and picked up the camera. He briefly considered using the camera to smash what still remained intact of the reporter's face. He raised the camera up, and as he did, he spotted a portrait of Katherine out of the corner of his eye.

Tony stopped, took the memory card out of the camera and placed it in his back pocket. Tony then raised the camera back up. He could see the fear in the reporter's bloody face. Tony no longer felt rage, he felt pity.

By this time, Wood had caught up to him.

"Tony!" he shouted. "Don't do it. Let me handle this."

"I've got this under control," Tony said calmly. Then he brought the camera down with all his might, smashing it on the ground a few inches away from the reporter's head as the reporter screamed and cried. Tony stood up, spit on the reporter and walked out of the room.

Tony went into his son's room, sat on the bed and wept. Miss Cook waited briefly, then followed to comfort him. Wood called the police. The smell of urine filled the room as the frightened reporter lost control of his bladder.

Two uniformed officers arrived. Detective Thomas heard about a call from the Michaels residence and arrived a short time later. Wood explained to the officers and Detective Thomas what had happened. They searched the house and found a broken window which the reporter smashed to gain entry into the house. The police handcuffed the reporter, covered his bloody face and led him out to the squad car.

Wood insisted on pressing charges. Tony agreed. Thomas took a brief statement from everyone and left. Wood gave instructions to Tony and Miss Cook to finish with their list while he went outside to handle the press. The reporters outside were scrambling to get photographs and get ready to do live reports on the incident while still trying to figure out exactly what happened.

"Ladies and Gentlemen," Wood shouted, "if I can have your attention. My name is Jake Wood. I am the attorney for Mr. Michaels. I will give you all a moment to get ready, and then I will address everyone at one time to explain what you have just seen."

Everyone with a camera or a microphone all gathered together and Wood began.

"The man you saw you leave this house with police illegally entered the house, was trespassing and was caught stealing valuable items from the house. As you know, the law in this state allows a person to defend his home by any means necessary. My client could have legally killed this man in defense of his home and property. But he chose to show mercy because my client is not a killer. Police did not question, nor arrest my client because his actions today were within the law.

"My client is innocent of the charges he is currently facing. Today, his actions were natural reactions that many of us would have taken under the same circumstances. This man violated my client's house and personal property, yet my client chose to let him walk out of this house alive, which we all know would not be the case in many houses in this state. This man today will be prosecuted to the full extent of the law.

"We understand the responsibilities of the jobs of those in the media, and we appreciate the work of all who do so with integrity and professionalism. My client is human. He has faults and weaknesses, as do we all. But he is not a killer. We hope you will present the events of the day as they happened and not anything more. We hope that you understand that my client is enduring a daunting reality of having his family stolen from him and being wrongly accused.

"My client today returned to his home for the first time since the incident that brought all of you to his front lawn. He returned to the place that should be his sanctuary, only to find it violated once again. My client has not had the chance to properly mourn the loss of his family, and today, a perfect opportunity to help in that process was stolen from him.

"We will not be answering any questions at this time, and we request that you allow my client some privacy. Thank you."

Reporters were shouting out questions but Wood silently walked back into the house. Tony and Miss Cook had finished their inventory of the house and were packing suitcases. Wood put a comforting hand on Tony's shoulder.

Wood's phone rang. It was Judge Randall wondering why Wood was just on the news. He threatened to revoke Tony's bail and demanded to see Wood and his client immediately.

"Yes, Your Honor," Wood said as he hung up the phone.

The three quickly finished packing the suitcases and took them downstairs to the garage. Tony looked around as Wood loaded the suitcases in his trunk.

"Give my tools away too," Tony said. "Maybe a school or

small business can use them. Or maybe a Scout troop. Sell the cars. I won't need one for a while, and if I get through this, I will want a new one."

Miss Cook jotted down some notes, and Wood pulled the car out of the garage. Tony sat in the backseat, staring at his feet, not acknowledging the throng of reporters yelling his name and shouting questions.

Wood was able to convince Judge Randall to not revoke Tony's bail. The judge agreed that his actions were legal and understandable given the situation. But he reminded Tony that this behavior brought unnecessary attention upon him, and if he could not avoid the spotlight, Judge Randall would indeed revoke the bail. This was Tony's last chance. Tony promised he wouldn't leave his hotel except to go to court or Wood's office or for his psych appointments.

Wood sent a crew that afternoon to pick up everything on Tony's list. It was brought to Wood's office where everything was inventoried. Tony grabbed a few items and took them to his hotel room. Angelique later asked for a few items and was allowed to take them to her apartment. One of the items was Tony's Rose Bowl jersey. She wore it nearly every day, needing to keep something of Tony's close to her.

Everything else was packed, labeled and placed in a storage unit that Wood kept. The following day, Wood sent a crew to pick up everything else and drop it off at local charities. The cars were sold to a dealership owned by a man Wood had successfully defended following his arrest on DUI charges.

Wood then contacted a realtor he knew who agreed to list the house. Tony was wary of having any open houses, thinking that would just attract reporters and weirdos rather than people actually looking to buy a house. The realtor listed the house based on comps, but let Tony know to expect lowball offers based on what had happened at the house. The realtor explained that if he lowered the asking price, people would just lowball that number. He also warned Tony that it might take a long time to get any serious interest since everything was still so fresh.

Surprisingly, it only took a day to receive an offer at the asking price, from a man in California. Tony was incredulous so he did a Google search on the man making the offer. It turned out that the man was very into the Goth scene. He was a former hacker who made money working Web security for various companies during the dot-com boom. He then developed his own software and started his own company which he later sold for millions.

Currently, the man was running two Web sites. One was an online store for all things Goth: clothing, makeup, accessories, etc. The other site was a porn site with very dark themes. There were no snuff films or any violence, mostly sex acts performed in coffins, cemeteries and other macabre places. Tony was a little disturbed that such a market existed and quite a bit disturbed at the thought of what such a Web site might want to do with his house. He quickly rejected the offer.

The next day the man made a counterproposal that was three times the market value for the house, in cash. Tony thought back to that first picnic he and Katherine had in the backyard, the proposal and all the happy memories from the early years of their marriage. He then imagined what might happen if he sold it. Tony finally decided that nothing could happen that was worse than what had already happened. He would never visit the site and would never know what they did. Tony was also worried that if he turned it down, he would never get another offer, so he finally accepted.

Once the deal was finalized, Tony took half of the money and set up an account for Angelique. He figured she could use the money to buy a house of her own if she wanted. She could leave town and start a new life if she wanted. Whatever she decided, it should more than cover her expenses so that she would not have to find a job until she was ready. Once the trial was over, Tony could decide what to do with the rest of the money, although it would certainly help pay his final hotel bill.

Tony was relieved that part of this ordeal was now over. There would be no more worries or distractions until the trial. Wood "accidentally" set up meetings with Tony and Angelique at the same time one day and let the two spend some time together alone in his small conference room. Angelique had dyed her hair a dark brown and was now straightening it. Tony thought it would take some getting used to, but she still looked gorgeous.

"I know you didn't do this, Tony," Angelique said trying to sound upbeat. "But please just say it to me anyway. And please tell me everything is going to be okay, even if you have to lie to say it."

Tony hugged Angelique and pulled back to look into her beautiful blue eyes.

"I would have never hurt them," he said. "And I never would have done anything to jeopardize my relationship with you. I have no idea what happened or who could have done this. I'm devastated by it, and I miss you so much."

"I miss you too," said Angelique. "I've hardly left the apartment since you were arrested. I'm going crazy not knowing what to do here. I get angry, then I get sad, then I get angry again. I totally screamed at some old lady at the grocery store this morning. I don't think I can go back to that store anymore."

They both laughed. It felt good. Neither had done that in a while.

"Hey, Tony, Mr. Wood told me about the house and the money you set aside for me," Angelique said being serious once again. "It's way too generous of you. I will never be able to thank you enough."

"You can thank me by staying by my side," Tony said. "You have been the best thing that ever happened to me. Don't worry about the money. If I ever get released, it's all going to be yours anyway."

"I'm not going anywhere without you," Angelique said with smile. She kissed Tony softly. "And please don't say the word 'if.' We both need to stay positive. Now let's talk about other things; let's pretend we're anywhere else but here. Okay?"

The two talked for hours, laughing and smiling as often as they could. For a little while the cold, dark reality of the situation was gone. Tony tried to enjoy and memorize every moment, knowing he may get very few chances like this again.

In the pretrial evidentiary hearing, Wood successfully argued to make sure the video of Tony's arrest and striking of the police officer would not be admissible in court. Tony watched it and still couldn't remember or believe it had happened. There it was though, filmed by his former colleagues at Channel 9.

Wood knew that when the jury was selected, it was likely whoever made the final twelve would have already seen it multiple times and probably formed some kind of opinion based off that. Wood could do nothing about that, but he could prevent them from seeing it again.

Wood also successfully argued that the attack on the reporter could not be used to prejudice the jury into thinking Tony was a violent man. Again, he knew that the potential jurors had likely heard about the incident and despite what he said to reporters that day, he knew it would not make Tony look very good in court.

It wouldn't matter that Tony's actions were legal. It wouldn't matter that the reporter made a plea deal to avoid federal prison and was serving a 23-month jail sentence, the first six weeks of which would be served in the infirmary with his jaw wired shut. Even though Tony's actions were legal and justifiable, the damage he had caused was severe and Wood didn't want anyone thinking about that once the trial began.

Wood was also able to convince the judge to ban cameras in the courtroom. He was hoping to ban all media, but Judge Randall disagreed on that point so Wood settled for the camera ban.

The prosecution had very little to say, feeling very confident in its case.

The judge ended the hearing and set a date for jury selection to begin.

William H. Gunderson III had debated whether to appear on television as a legal expert on the Michaels case. He had done so many times before on other cases, but now he was preparing to run for governor of Texas. He wasn't sure how long the trial would last. He wasn't sure if the exposure was the right forum, but his team convinced him that keeping his face in the public would be a good thing. It wasn't a tough sell as Gunderson was fascinated by this case and wanted to be in on all the details of the trial.

Gunderson had more wealth than he could ever need, but he never worked cheaply for anything. CNN offered him the most money for his exclusive insights and agreed to release him from his duties if the trial extended past the date to declare his candidacy for governor.

To gain more publicity and exposure and to gain positive momentum, over the next few months Gunderson would do several things to improve his odds when it was time to campaign. He personally paid to have two churches rebuilt in Galveston that were destroyed by a hurricane. He rebuilt a church damaged by fire in Midland. He donated enough money to build a new children's hospital in Arlington. And he funded endowments for scholarships at several universities throughout the state. Gunderson figured all that, along with the facial and name recognition gained by this high-profile case, would put him over the top.

One of Gunderson's appeals to CNN was that he had worked on both prosecution and defense and could offer insight from both perspectives. With the upcoming campaign, Gunderson decided that it was best early on to focus more on the prosecution, presenting an image of being tough on crime. It was a calculated choice with Gunderson believing he might be able to capture extra votes.

In his first report on CNN, he focused on the brutality of the murders. Surely, he suggested, only a person who knew the victims well could have committed murders of this type. He played up the fact that Tony had struck a police officer and busted up a reporter's face. Gunderson asserted that Tony Michaels was a violent, angry man who was indeed capable of such murders.

Gunderson also highlighted the cleanliness of the crime scene when police arrived. Michaels was the only one who could have cleaned up enough. Gunderson proclaimed, "If I was prosecuting this case, I would expect it to be a rather short trial. And I would expect it to end with Mr. Michaels getting the needle."

Jury selection began in normal fashion. The first pool of 150 potential jurors was called into the courtroom. The judge mentioned that it would be a murder trial and could take anywhere from a couple of weeks to a few months. The judge asked for potential jurors who could not sit on this case to explain their reasons.

The judge then asked if anybody felt that based on what they had seen or read about the case so far, if the potential jurors could remain unbiased and base their decision solely on the evidence presented in court. Those who thought they couldn't explained.

The judge then stated that because of the high-profile nature of this case, that any jurors selected would be sequestered for the entirety of the proceedings. Anyone who objected was asked to state their case.

The judge called a brief recess and whittled the list down to 47 people. The first panel of twelve was called to take their place in the jury box. The attorneys alternated asking the panel questions and excluding potential jurors until the final

twelve and alternates were decided upon. The jury consisted
of seven men and five women of diverse ethnicities and back-
grounds. Kevin Wilson, a veteran driver for UPS, volunteered
to be the foreman. The others were fine with Wilson leading
the group. The judge sent everyone to lunch and ordered that
all parties be back in court at 2 p.m. for opening statements.

Eric Joseph was the prosecutor assigned to the case, and
he began the proceedings.

"Ladies and Gentlemen of the jury, most of you probably
know the defendant from the Channel 9 news. Until recently,
you couldn't drive anywhere in the Metroplex without seeing
billboards proclaiming him to be 'The Most Trusted Man in
Texas,'" Joseph began, adding air quotes derisively.

"But this man, who we were all supposed to trust, cannot
be trusted. His wife couldn't trust him as he has admitted to
multiple infidelities. So every time you saw those billboards
and every time you watched the Channel 9 news, the defendant was lying to you.

"Lying and infidelity are not illegal, and that is not why we
are here today. No, unfortunately, we are here today because
the defendant murdered first his unborn child, then his young
son and finally his wife, all in a spectacularly brutal fashion.

"The defendant admits to being home alone with his family the night of the murders. According to both the defendant
and the evidence that will be presented in this case, nobody
else was in the their residence that night. The coroner put the
time of death at 3 a.m. Michaels admits to being home that
time with his pregnant wife and child sleeping. The defendant
claims he is innocent. How can we trust that?

"Remember that the defendant works in a profession

where he has spent countless hours rehearsing and delivering horrible news in a palatable fashion. He has spent countless hours in front of the mirror, practicing facial expressions so that he is able to smile even after informing you about a plane crash in which hundreds of people died. Keep that in mind if the defendant speaks in this trial or if you are watching him for reactions. Nothing about this man can be trusted.

"Over the course of this trial, we will prove the defendant is a violent narcissist who planned and carried out this heinous and despicable act. By the time this trial is over, I am confident that each and every one of you will neither trust the defendant nor his lawyer's magic tricks to distract you. I am confident that you will find the defendant guilty of three counts of capital murder. Thank you."

Joseph sat down. Wood stood up and began.

"Ladies and Gentlemen, despite what my counterpart says, my client can be trusted. I know he is innocent of these crimes. I believe that by the end of this trial, you will know that too.

"Mr. Michaels is not a perfect man. He is certainly flawed. He has certainly made mistakes in his life. But who among us has not? My client may not be perfect, but he is no murderer. He is devastated by the loss of his wife and children.

"The evidence the state has in this case is minimal and circumstantial at best. Forget whatever the prosecution says about his infidelities or anything else designed to besmirch his character. This trial is not about whether Mr. Michaels is a good guy. It's not about whether you would like to hang out with him or whether you would approve of him dating your sister or daughter. This trial is about the murder of three innocent victims.

"Mr. Michaels did not take the lives of his family; they were stolen from him. It is your responsibility to see through whatever media coverage you might have seen and ignore that. My counterpart claimed I would use magic tricks to distract you. I have no tricks, but our job in this courtroom is to persuade you. It is your responsibility to see through anything I might say or my counterpart might say and look ONLY to the facts of the case.

"If you can do that, I am confident you will find my client not guilty of these charges. Thank you."

With that, Judge Randall adjourned court until Monday at 10 a.m. The trial would begin then. The jury was led out and transported to where they were being sequestered.

The trial proceeded as expected with Joseph trying to overload the jury with the evidence while Wood tried to shoot holes in that evidence, doing everything he could to create doubt in the minds of the jurors. Angelique sat in the back of the courtroom in black every day. She made sure each day to make eye contact with Tony, but tried to remain as inconspicuous as possible. Katherine's parents did not appear in court.

The prosecution called CSI Lopez to the stand first. Then Dr. Long, the coroner. The jury was given all the grisly details, shown all the disturbing photographs. Others, including Mrs. Mitchell who had made the 911 call, were also brought to the stand during the first week as was Andy Patterson, the last person to speak to Tony Michaels before the murders.

Andy reluctantly took the stand and was sworn in.

"Mr. Patterson, you were with the defendant on the night of the murders, is that correct?" Joseph asked.

"Yes, I did my radio show, and then stuck around to have a few drinks."

"Will you describe his mood and his behavior for the court?"

"He was anxious, distracted, nervous. Definitely wasn't himself that night."

"What was he so nervous about?"

"He was thinking about asking Katherine for a divorce. He asked if I would think he was an asshole if he did. I told him yes, but he needed to do what was best for him."

"Was the defendant ever unfaithful to his wife?"

"Yes."

"How often?"

"Well, a couple of years ago, Tony had a chance to take a job in New York working for the network. In this business, you want to work in the biggest markets and get the most exposure. This job was as big as it gets. Katherine refused to go. It's the only time I've ever known them to fight. It lasted quite a while, and Tony had a moment of weakness. He apologized that night, she forgave him and they moved forward."

"Was that the only time?"

"No. He helped a college student get an internship at Channel 9, and they got a little too close and started sleeping together."

"Did he apologize that time?"

"Not that I'm aware of."

"Why did he say he wanted a divorce?"

"Well, there was another potential job opening. He knew Katherine wasn't going to ever leave the area, and he didn't think he could stay with somebody who was holding him back. He wanted a new opportunity, and he knew he would never get it if he stayed with her."

"Mr. Michaels was worth a lot of money," Joseph continued. "So I imagine a divorce would have cost him quite a bit of money."

"Tony didn't ever care about the money. He said he wanted Katherine to have the house and however much she needed. He was fine with whatever was left."

"I don't know, Mr. Patterson. She was holding him back in his career, she obviously wasn't satisfying him sexually or he wouldn't have needed to stray and a divorce would have cost him millions of dollars. That certainly seems like motive to me."

"Objection!" shouted Wood.

"Sustained," ruled Judge Randall. "The jury will please disregard that last comment from Mr. Joseph."

"Mr. Patterson," Joseph said, not skipping a beat, "have you ever seen the defendant get violent?"

"Only once," answered Andy, curious how the prosecution knew or if Joseph was simply fishing with the question.

"Can you describe that incident for the court, please?"

"Well, it was the weekend before school started one year and we were having a big party at the fraternity house. Tony never drank during football season so he was sober that night. There were some incoming freshman at the party, their first big college party. As the night wore on, we noticed this guy had a girl pinned up against the wall, and she clearly wasn't enjoying it. He had his hand up her top and she was struggling to fend him off.

"A lot of us wanted to do something, but Tony was the one

who stepped up," Andy continued. "He asked the girl if she was okay. She said no. Tony politely asked the kid to stop. The kid told Tony to fuck off and mind his own business. Tony told the kid if he didn't take his hand off her chest, he was going to rip that hand off and bitch slap him with his own hand until he cried. The kid took his hand off her, said something vulgar and spit in Tony's face."

"What happened next?" asked Joseph.

"Tony punched the guy so hard his face caved in like it was made out of clay or something. The dude somehow got up and just walked out of the house."

"His face caved in?"

"Yeah, it was pretty gross. He busted up his cheek and eye socket. I don't know how the guy managed to walk out."

"No further questions," said Joseph.

"Did Tony ever face any charges from the police over this?" Wood asked immediately. "Was he punished by the school or the football team in any way?"

"No," Andy said. "Somebody found the kid passed out in the street a few blocks away and called an ambulance. We heard by then he was a swollen, bloody mess. He told the paramedics that he had too much to drink and fell and hit his face on the curb. I think he knew if he put it on Tony, he would face sexual assault charges, and Tony would come out looking like a hero. His face was pretty busted up, though. He needed a few surgeries. He dropped out of school and moved away."

"What happened to the girl?"

"It was crazy. The next day the girl, her name was Marita, she showed up with I'm guessing about 200 cookies. All different kinds because she wasn't sure what Tony's favorite was.

After that, Marita was always at the house. She was so cute and so much fun and she clearly wanted Tony. For a while she followed him around like a puppy. She really looked after him when he had his knee surgery. For some reason he looked at her more like a little sister and just wanted to protect her. The rest of us all had a crush on Marita, I mean, you couldn't help it. She had an awesome personality and a fantastic body. But I think we were all afraid of Tony."

"What do you mean people were afraid of Tony?" asked Wood.

"It's not so much that we were afraid of him, but he was very protective of Marita," Andy replied. "One of the guys made a crude comment about her once. Tony calmly reminded us of what happened the last time somebody was rude to her. After that, we all started thinking of her as more of a little sister. When she gave up on the idea of dating Tony, she started having dates pick her up at the house instead of her apartment. We made it pretty intimidating for them. Scared a few off until she found a really nice guy that we all approved of. They ended up getting married, and she even asked Tony to give her away at the wedding."

"So Tony was only violent to protect others?"

"Yeah, I mean, a bunch of college football players and fraternity boys. Things got rowdy from time to time. But Tony was always the cool one. He had this quality about him where everybody always listened. That's what made him such a great leader on the football team and such a great anchor. No matter how big the skirmish got, Tony was always the peacemaker and always got things calmed down before it escalated too much."

"One last question, Mr. Patterson," Wood said, pausing. "What was the last thing Tony said to you the night his wife was killed?"

"He told me he was going to leave Dallas once the divorce was final. He made me promise to look after Katherine for him. He made me promise I would check in on her and make sure she was okay and to call him if she or the kids needed anything."

"Thank you, Andy," Wood said. "No further questions."

"Mr. Patterson," Joseph immediately responded, "you saw this man, in your words, 'cave a man's face in,' and with all the reasons in the world to get Mrs. Michaels out of the way you want us to believe that he wanted to protect her?"

"Yes."

"Clearly he can be violent and overreact to situations even when sober. It's not much of a stretch to think that the defendant asked for a divorce, his wife objected and he went crazy."

"Objection!" shouted Wood once again.

"Sustained," Judge Randall agreed. "Strike that last statement from the records, and, jury, disregard the comment. Counselor, if you have any further questions you may proceed. Otherwise, save those remarks for your closing argument."

"Sorry, Your Honor," Joseph replied. "Mr. Patterson, after seeing such a violent act while sober and with only a little provocation, what makes you certain that with years of marital strife the defendant would not have been capable of so much more, especially with his judgment impaired by alcohol?"

"It's just like with Marita," Andy said. "Tony was always the protective one. He was like that with everybody. He was always looking out for people, especially women. Tony has made his share of mistakes, but he is a kind man. If you ever saw him around TJ, he was the gentlest father I've ever seen. Now if Tony had woken up, found whoever did this, he would have protected his family. If that happened, I would believe anything that might have happened after that. But no way would he hurt his family."

"No further questions," Joseph said with a slight hint of temporary resignation.

On the Monday of week two, the prosecution called its final witness, Detective Thomas.

Joseph led Thomas through a series of questions allowing Thomas to set the scene that evening, to paint of picture of everything he saw and didn't see. Thomas described the evidence and his conversations with the coroner, the crime lab, the neighbors and Mr. Michaels himself.

Finally it was Wood's turn to question Thomas. He knew the case potentially hinged on his cross-examination.

"Detective Thomas, did you ever have any doubts during this investigation?"

"Doubts?" Thomas asked, knowing he had several doubts throughout the investigation. All the evidence pointed toward Tony, but the doubts remained. He wanted to be sure to help the case but not perjure himself in the process.

"Yes. Doubts, questions? My client said when you spoke, he thought you believed his story."

"I believe your client misspoke," Thomas answered strongly. "I told him I would do everything I could to make sure whoever did this would pay for it. If he was telling the truth I wanted to find out, if he was lying I wanted to find out. Unfortunately for him, all the evidence in this case points at one person. That's the defendant, that's why you're here today and not another lawyer with another client."

"You say all the evidence pointed toward my client, but you weren't surprised at how little evidence you found."

"No. Why would I be surprised?" Thomas asked. "I couldn't even tell you how many crime scenes I have been to. These murders were committed by one cold cat. Mr. Michaels had plenty of time to clean up. Did a pretty good job too, just missed a few things like his ring, the saw and he let the fire burn out before it got all of his sweatshirt."

"Detective, my client had quite a bit to drink the night of the murders, enough to make him vomit. Do you really believe he could have done all this while severely inebriated?"

"Well, as far as the alcohol goes, we all have different tolerances. I don't know his prior history; maybe he could function just fine. I mean, he drove home without hitting anything or drawing any attention to himself, so he is either incredibly lucky or was not as impaired as you say.

"As for the vomit, there was no evidence of that at the house," Thomas continued. "Either he has the cleanest vomit ever or he was well enough to do a great job of cleaning up after himself. It's also possible if he did vomit it was not due to the drinking but rather a reaction to what he saw and did. I mean, my boy who arrived at the scene first, he threw up when he saw the bodies. So to answer your question, there was no evidence to suggest he was at all impaired."

Undeterred, Wood went on, trying to attack the evidence.

"Detective Thomas, Mrs. Michaels was amputated at both ankles, both knees, both hips, both wrists, both elbows, both shoulders and she was decapitated. That's thirteen different places where she was dismembered. Tony Jr. was amputated at both thighs and at both shoulders. That's another four. Doesn't it strike you as odd that there wasn't more blood?"

"To be honest, no."

"Please explain."

"Well, when somebody kills somebody in the heat of the moment, they are usually pretty sloppy about the killing and sloppy in the cleanup. But when it's premeditated and you have the time to plan it, a smart person would plan the cleanup as well. The defendant is a smart man, has a degree from Northwestern. That's not an easy school to get in. He would have had a plan to get away with it. Maybe he had put drop cloths all over the garage or collected the blood in those five-gallon buckets you can get at any hardware store. That would have minimized the evidence."

"Did you find any drop cloths or buckets in your search of the house?"

"No."

"Did you find any in his trash or in the trash of any of the houses on his street that you searched?"

"No."

"Anything in his car?"

"No."

"What about work?"

"We didn't find anything outside the house, but he must have passed a thousand dumpsters between his house and work. He could have dumped it in any one of them. There's no way we could search every dumpster between Plano and downtown Dallas. If he was smart, he would have had something in his car too so no evidence was left there."

"There's something else, Detective, that makes me curious," Wood said.

"Sure. Go."

"Mrs. Michaels was five months pregnant, but she still did yoga on a regular basis and did some strength training and cardio work on a limited basis since her pregnancy, but avidly prior to that. She was a healthy, fit, strong woman. More than half of the dismemberments occurred while she was still alive. She had no defensive wounds, no bruises, no DNA under her fingernails, no ligature marks, no drugs or alcohol in her system and upon my client's arrest, he showed no signs of a struggle on his body. Is that correct?"

"Yes, that is correct."

"So are you saying that a strong, healthy woman would just allow her body to be mutilated without putting up a fight?"

"Objection, Your Honor!" Joseph shouted.

"Overruled," the judge replied.

"Look, on the surface it seems crazy, but there are plenty of possible explanations. Usually when multiple members of a family are killed in a single incident the perpetrator starts with the biggest threat, which would have been Mr. Michaels in this case. Most people would have killed him first, then Mrs. Michaels and then the boy. But Mr. Michaels wasn't harmed at all. If, as you want people to believe, he is innocent, then that is the most unbelievable part of this whole incident.

"As far as her body having no marks, maybe she was paralyzed by fear. Maybe she was under the influence of something. The people in our lab are top-notch and always on point, but not all drugs are detectable. Some will knock you out but not stay in your body long. Your client is a wealthy man. He could have acquired something like that.

"And you mentioned that she was dismembered in thirteen different places. All those wounds were cauterized. What makes you think a smart man like your client wouldn't have restrained her, and then used the cuts and the burning to obscure any marks left by the restraints? That's my explanation."

"So if my client went through all this trouble to cover his tracks, why would he leave the bodies outside to be found?"

"Objection, speculative," Joseph shouted.

"Nah, I'll answer," Thomas said before Judge Randall could rule. "You would have to ask your client to know the real answer. But if you want me to think of reasons, maybe it was remorse after the fact. Maybe he wanted to get caught. Maybe he couldn't sleep with them in the house. Or maybe he just didn't think anybody would find them before he could do whatever he had eventually intended with the bodies. I mean, if a little boy could throw a football better, we might all be somewhere else right now."

With that, Wood relented. The prosecution rested. The judge adjourned court until Thursday, when the defense would get its chance to state its case.

For its first witness, the defense called Greta, Tony's waitress at Hooters on the night of the murders.

"May I call you Greta, miss?" Wood asked politely.

"Of course!"

"Now, Greta, please state your occupation and place of employment."

"Yes, sir, I am a Hooter Girl," Greta said proudly. "I work

at the Plano restaurant. I am a theater major at UT-Dallas, and I am in this year's Hooters calendar."

"And were you working on the night of January 5th?"

"Yes," said Greta with her warm smile. "I remember that night because the Cowboys radio show was at our restaurant that night. Because it was the playoffs, the place was packed. I also remember it because the next day the cops came by."

Wood pointed at his client, asking, "Do you recognize this man?"

"I do. He sat in my section that night. He's really handsome, and I was trying to be flirty, but at first he seemed very distracted and upset. I had to work really hard to get him to smile and talk a little."

"Did he mention anything that was bothering him?"

"No, he didn't. He barely said anything at first. Most guys pay a lot of attention to the girls or the sports on TV or play with their phone. He was just staring at the table like his dog had died. Oh my gosh, I should not have said that. I'm so sorry."

"It's quite all right, Greta. Did my client eventually lighten up?"

"Yeah, I eventually broke him down, and we talked a little bit. His friend, the radio guy, bought a couple shots of tequila for him, and then he started to be pretty fun. We mostly talked about hockey until the show started. Then I got busy, but we talked a little bit more later. He was really sweet, and he left me a great tip!"

"Did he have a lot to drink that night?"

"Oh my gosh, he did," Greta said apologetically. "It was Wednesday, so we had our $1.99 pints all night. I liked him, and he was an easy table. I didn't want him to leave so I kept bringing him new pints. I did get a little worried at one point, but when the radio show was over, his friend joined him and mentioned getting a cab, so I assumed they were splitting one."

"And how much exactly did he have that night?"

"He had fifteen pints, and his friend bought him a few shots. I was surprised at the end of the night when I printed out his check. I remember it came out to $40-something with his food. He gave me a hundred-dollar bill and told me the rest was my tip. I brought his change back, and he insisted I keep it. I told him he must be drunk and didn't know what he was doing. I tried to slip a twenty in his sweatshirt pocket, but he stopped me. He said I cheered him up, which he really needed, and that's what the extra was for."

"So he had fifteen pints of beer, and by a few shots, do you mean three?"

"I think it was at least four, maybe five," said Greta, starting to feel embarrassed as she was realizing how much alcohol she had actually served him. "I don't know how he did it."

"Thank you, miss," Wood said to Greta, then turned to Joseph and said, "Your witness."

"Now, Miss Greta," Joseph started, sounding like a true Southern gentleman, "did you have any concerns that you were overserving the defendant? Was he acting impaired in any way?"

"Well, now that we talk about it, it sounds like way too much," Greta said, the smile now gone. "But at the time, I couldn't tell. It was really busy, so I wasn't paying as much attention as I should have, but at one point I started to watch him more closely to see if I needed to cut him off or get him some water or coffee. But he never slurred his speech, he never stumbled off his stool and he walked normal when he went to the restroom. I even had my manager Brian go check on him. He went to talk to him for a while and said he seemed fine. He said I could keep serving him."

"So this man drank all that alcohol and showed no signs of intoxication that neither you nor your manager felt the need to cut him off? Knowing the potential liabilities your restaurant could face, your manager told you to keep serving him?"

"That is correct."

"Thank you, Miss Greta. No further questions."

The defense continued to call witnesses through Friday and into Monday. Wood debated putting Tony on the stand the whole time. But he knew Tony would not do well under cross-examination.

Wood's final witness was Dr. Aaron Baldwin, who specialized in internal medicine and was now teaching at UT Southwestern Medical School in Dallas. One of the courses he taught was on the effects of alcohol on the human body.

Wood had the doctor introduce himself to the court.

"Doctor Baldwin, I don't want to brag for you, but weren't you on the cover of *D Magazine* a few years ago as the best doctor in the state?"

"Yes. That was before I gave up my practice and decided to teach instead."

"As I understand it, UT Southwestern is the top-ranked medical school in the state. Is that correct?"

"I suppose it depends who you ask, but several publications have ranked us in the Top Twenty nationally and No. 1 in the state."

"And what do you teach there?"

"My practice was in internal medicine so I teach various courses. The last three years I have been teaching a course about the effects of alcohol on the body."

"Now my client weighs 215 pounds. If he were to arrive at a bar at 5 o'clock, drink fifteen pints of beer and four or five shots of tequila, what do you think his blood alcohol content would be at, say, midnight and again at three in the morning?"

The doctor pondered and did some quick calculations.

"Fifteen pints is the equivalent of twenty 12-ounce beers. At that weight, give or take, he should be roughly at .35 percent at midnight and down to about a .30 by 3 o'clock."

"That's four times the legal limit," Wood said. "What kind of behavior would you expect from a person at .35 percent?"

"Honestly, I wouldn't expect much behavior at all. That amount of alcohol is roughly the equivalent of surgical anesthesia. It's past the point of alcohol poisoning. I would be surprised to find somebody still functioning at any level with that much alcohol in their system. I would expect vomiting and I would expect the subject to be passed out. In the emergency room, I have seen patients slip into a coma at .35."

"Thank you, Doctor," Wood said, turning the witness over to his counterpart.

Joseph was eager to cross-examine the doctor.

"Doctor, if I took a group of twenty random men, all weighing 215 pounds, and gave them all equal amounts of alcohol, would the effects be identical?"

"In terms of the blood alcohol content, they would be nearly identical. In terms of behavior, it could vary greatly depending on each individual's medical conditions, medications, drinking history, mood and how much they had to eat that day."

"So while it may be unlikely, is it possible for a man with a .35 to function?"

"It's possible. You have probably heard the term 'functioning alcoholic.' If an individual uses a substance, be it alcohol, cocaine, etc., enough, he will build up a tolerance. It then takes more and more to achieve the desired effect. The alcohol will do the same amount of damage to the liver and kidneys, but outwardly, some people can operate without noticeable impairment at a level that might kill you or me."

"Thank you, Doctor. I have no further questions."

Wood began his follow-up.

"Let me ask you this, if the individual in question did much of that drinking late in the evening, finishing with a few shots, wouldn't it take some time for his blood alcohol to rise?"

"It would take a little time, and possibly be slowed if he had a full stomach, but the peak would be dramatic."

"So it's possible he could do a couple of quick shots at last call and be legally drunk, but not necessarily visibly impaired. Then when he gets home 10 minutes later, feel the full effect of the alcohol?"

"Yes, it is possible. The individual should definitely not be driving. If he somehow managed to make it home unscathed, I would not expect him to be conscious very long. At the least, the majority of people would have some vomiting and pass out. As I said before, it's possible he could suffer much worse."

"Dr. Baldwin, even if this individual managed to make it home safely, wouldn't he have some impairment?" Wood asked.

"Even if the individual didn't show many of the signs we associate with intoxication, such as slurred speech, staggering, etc., there would be a loss in motor function, for sure," Dr. Baldwin stated.

"Doctor, have you seen the photos of the victims?"

"Yes, unfortunately, I have."

"Now in your expert opinion, could a man who had such a large quantity of alcohol have made those cuts on the victims? Could he have done so much cutting without getting himself injured? Could he have cauterized the wounds safely and without burning himself?"

"I don't think it's possible," Dr. Baldwin said. "The cuts are very precise, very clean and very straight. I would expect hesitation marks or the cuts to be irregular. I would be amazed if he could operate power tools without injuring himself while that intoxicated. I didn't see what was used to cauterize the wounds, but I can't imagine he could do that much without suffering some serious burns himself."

"Thanks again, Doctor. No further questions."

With no more witnesses, the defense rested. Court was adjourned until 10 o'clock Tuesday morning, at which time final arguments would be heard.

Tony searched the crowd for Angelique. When he made eye contact he flashed what he wanted desperately to be a hopeful-looking smile. She smiled back, showed him her crossed fingers and blew him a kiss.

Tony then had a brief conversation with William H. Gunderson III. He wasn't sure why, but he took his card. Tony found it odd that Gunderson would seek him out or offer his card. Gunderson had only recently started to go by "Bill" in an effort to sound more like a man of the people. He hadn't been in a courtroom in years. Tony wasn't paying any attention to the news, and even he knew the Republican Party was preparing "Bill" to run for governor.

Tony found Wood and the two went back to Wood's office. Tony attempted to hide the fear but to no avail. The two discussed the case and closing argument.

"Look, if we lose I won't blame you," Tony said. "You worked your butt off, and I'm grateful for what you have done, especially helping Angelique. Promise me you will keep in touch with her if I go away. She means everything to me."

"Don't go admitting defeat just yet," Wood said. "I'll admit that when I first took this case, I wasn't sure it was winnable. But we have taken some big swings, and we'll take one more tomorrow. Sure we took some blows along the way, but don't give up."

Tony nodded.

"If you do lose, definitely appeal," Wood said. "If you lose that one, appeal that too. Don't let them kill an innocent man. I know you didn't do this. I don't know if have convinced enough jurors, but promise me you will appeal if we lose. I will fight for you as long as you want me to. If you think somebody else might be better, I'll step aside, but I'll stay in your corner until we find whatever answers we still need to find."

Tony gave Wood a hug and headed out of the office. Miss Cook was waiting to take him back to the hotel. They drove in silence. She always walked him to his room.

"There's no need to walk me back to the room," Tony said while waiting for the elevator. "I'll be fine."

"For what it's worth, I believe you," Miss Cook said. "You're a good man. Stay strong."

Miss Cook hugged Tony and held him until the elevator arrived. Tony later met with the concierge asking him to find a good scotch before he returned from court the next day.

Tony sat quietly in his room, staring a hole in the wall that night and barely slept as his mind raced. He had grown used to these four wall surrounding him. He wondered how many nights he had left here. Would he be able to grow used to a different set of walls, much less comfortable and posh? He cried for Katherine and TJ. He cried for Angelique. When he did sleep, the faceless smile still haunted his dreams and startled him awake.

Angelique had avoided watching any news since Tony was arrested. But with closing arguments tomorrow, she was curious what people were saying. She turned on CNN and saw William H. "Bill" Gunderson with the title "Legal Expert" under his name.

"I believe the defense did not live up to its end of the bargain in this case," Gunderson said to the host, Frank Sanchez. "Based on the evidence as I heard it in court, there were a lot of questions that simply weren't asked here. There are a lot of questions I have in my head and a lot of doubt about the evidence. I don't believe those questions were asked or answered."

"Mr. Gunderson, you've said from the beginning that you believed Mr. Michaels was guilty," the host said. "Is that no longer the case?"

"I apologize for correcting you, Frank," Gunderson responded. "What I said from the beginning was that if I was the prosecutor in this case, I believe it would go quickly and end with Michaels getting the needle. I believe the way the case was presented to the jury, we will see a guilty verdict in the next few days.

"I do have concerns, though, having also worked on the side of the defense," Gunderson continued. "I think there are enough holes in the evidence that I would have created enough doubt that we could see a different verdict."

"So are you saying he is guilty or not guilty?"

"I am saying that based on the court proceedings, he will be found guilty," Gunderson replied. "Based on my experience working both sides of the room, I have far too many questions about the evidence that the defense did not question. They certainly tried to poke holes, but they used a small needle to poke those holes. I would have tried a much-stronger approach. I would have been poking holes big enough to walk through."

"Maybe I'm just not quite following you," Sanchez said.

"Frank, the evidence is the evidence," Gunderson answered. "You can't get around that. But you can interpret different things from it. It's not just about what you see, but also about how you see it and what you don't see as well. Guilt or innocence is all in the eye of the beholder. It's the attorney's job to present the case in a way where the jury can only see one thing.

"The evidence shown in court suggests Mr. Michaels is guilty," Gunderson continued. "But what I did not see suggests to me that the killings may not have even taken place at the Michaels residence. I think the victims were taken elsewhere, and then the bodies returned later."

"What makes you say that?" Sanchez inquired.

"Well, again, it's simply the way I see things, and what I don't see," Gunderson said. "I just have my doubts. Based on the trial, I'm not sure the jurors will have those same doubts."

"Are you trying to create that doubt?"

"No, that's not my job," Gunderson said smugly. "You have asked *for my opinion on the case. I believe if I was prosecuting Mr. Michaels, he would be executed. I believe if I was defending him, he would be a free man in a few days. But I'm not defending him. And I am not here to build a case for his appeal. I am just here giving my opinions. It's not to disparage his legal team. I just see the case could have potentially turned out differently."*

"Mr. Gunderson," Sanchez interrupted, "you have been a staunch supporter of the death penalty and the rumors swirl that you will be running for political office soon. Are you saying you would want Mr. Michaels to walk free following this terrible tragedy?"

"Frank, I apologize if you are unable to follow my logic," Gunderson said with as much condescension as possible. "I absolutely do believe in the death penalty. I don't believe the taxpayers should have to pay room and board and medical expenses for those who clearly contribute nothing to society and only take.

"If Mr. Michaels did commit this atrocity against his family," Gunderson continued, "there is no punishment severe enough. As a society we cannot let these things happen without responding harshly. I just believe that the defense did not place enough of a burden on the prosecution which could have definitively answered the question of guilty or not guilty. I still have questions that I would like answered. I would hate to see an innocent man be put to death just as much as I would hate to see justice not being served for these poor victims."

"So what should we expect?" Sanchez asked.

"Personally, I expect closing arguments where each side will passionately support their argument," Gunderson said. "I expect the jury will take a few days to deliberate and most likely return with a guilty verdict. I expect the defendant to appeal the verdict, and I expect your network to provide a more competent host the next time I am asked to provide my opinion."

With that, Gunderson turned off the feed from his office and headed out to dinner with his wife.

Tuesday morning, Tony was finally asleep when somebody was trying to nudge him awake. It was Miss Cook. Tony had turned off his alarm, and then fallen back asleep.

"Mr. Michaels! Mr. Michaels!" Miss Cook was saying as loud as she thought she could without disturbing anyone in the next room. "You need to wake up. This is a big day. We can't be late."

Dazed and weary, Tony sat up. Miss Cook leaned down to his level and put her hands on his shoulders.

"Mr. Michaels," Miss Cook said trying to be simultaneously pleasant and stern, "we need to leave very quickly. I need you to take a quick shower. Skip the shaving. I will pick out a suit for you and make some coffee."

Tony took a quick shower, threw some gel in his hair, ran his fingers through his hair a few times and decided that would do for today. Miss Cook helped him hurriedly dress and she tied his tie for him as he drank his coffee.

"There, all set!" she said with a smile. "You look handsome and innocent!"

Tony was still in a daze. Had he ever seen Miss Cook smile? He had no words, just a nod. She kissed him on the cheek.

"For luck!" she said. "Now, we must go."

Tony was in a complete fog in court. He wasn't sure if it was the lack of sleep catching up to him or if it was the realization that twelve men and women were about to decide if he should live or die. Tony hadn't looked at the jury box at all during the trial. He looked at the judge, his lawyer, the witnesses and occasionally the table in front of him.

Today he tried to examine the eyes and the faces of the people who were going to decide his fate. He didn't hear a word either attorney said in their closing arguments. He didn't hear the judge give his instructions to the jury. He didn't even hear the bailiff say, "All rise!" Wood had to tap Tony on the shoulder to get his attention.

Tony searched for Angelique. He tried, but couldn't muster a smile. She blew him a kiss and mouthed the words, "I love you," as Wood led him out of the courtroom.

Wood ordered lunch back at his office, but Tony wasn't hungry. He went into a spare room with a couch and took a nap. He slept for a few hours feeling more refreshed and Miss Cook took him back to the hotel where he started drinking for the first time since the murders.

Tony woke up Wednesday morning with a hangover. As smooth as the $500 bottle of Macallan was, Tony had a little too much and having been sober since the murders, it hit him hard. He checked his phone. There were no messages. He got himself together and headed downstairs to eat.

Tony ate breakfast. He was hoping the caffeine from the coffee and the ibuprofen would chase the headache away quickly. His mind was racing. He thought about staying drunk until the verdict was read. He debated whether he could survive more trials if he was found guilty and decided to appeal.

Tony had never been one to quit, but the idea of reliving his nightmare over and over again seemed unbearable. He had been able to stay in a luxurious hotel during the trial, but during the appeals process he would be in prison, and he wasn't sure if he could survive that. Even staying in the hotel for as long as he had was playing tricks on his mind. At least in the hotel he could watch movies, order room service, go downstairs to eat, work out. In prison he would just be hoping to get through each day without being beaten or raped or hanging himself.

Tony went back to his room. He later ordered a burger and some beers. He turned on the television and watched the story of an innocent man sentenced to life in prison for allegedly murdering his wife. Tony watched and knew there would be no escape for him. He decided the needle would be preferable to life in prison. He debated if he would even appeal. The needle would bring an end to the nightmares, even if it didn't bring justice.

Then he thought of Angelique. She had stood by his side throughout the ordeal and never wavered. He had to make an effort for her. He looked for the card that Gunderson had given him after closing arguments but couldn't find it. He remembered dropping it on the floor. Perhaps the maids had thrown it out with the trash.

No big deal, he thought. Gunderson's number shouldn't be too hard to find. At the very least, he could get his office number and leave a message.

Tony found the office number and spoke with a woman named Susan, Gunderson's secretary. Susan told Tony that Gunderson was not in, but he had been expecting his call. She gave him Gunderson's mobile number. Tony called and got Gunderson's voice mail. Later, Gunderson called back to let Tony know he had a charity function to attend that evening but would be happy to meet with him Thursday evening. Gunderson suggested 6 o'clock. Tony agreed.

Tony spent Thursday restless. He checked his phone every

few minutes for any calls or messages. His mind was still racing with questions he couldn't possibly answer. How long would the jury take? The longer they take, is that a good sign or a bad omen? The questions kept coming. Tony wanted to go for a run, but he remembered the day he found out Katherine was pregnant when he ran until he collapsed. That killed the idea of running.

More questions? Had the blow to the head changed him? Was it possible it caused something to snap inside him to actually commit the crimes he was accused of? He had never really gotten over the lost New York opportunity. Maybe Katherine woke up in the middle of the night and they started to argue. Even on his heaviest drinking nights, he couldn't remember sleeping much past 10 o'clock. Something must have happened for him to sleep well into the afternoon. Or was this just the room playing tricks on him?

It didn't seem possible, but Tony was no longer certain of what was real and what wasn't. Wow, he really wanted to drink, but whatever Gunderson had to say would be wasted if Tony was drunk so he convinced himself to abstain.

The minutes dragged by at a snail's pace. At four o'clock Tony received a text from Wood. "No verdict today. Hang in there. Stay positive."

How was it only four o'clock? It felt like it must be Saturday by now. Still two hours to wait for Gunderson. A drink or two might calm Tony's nerves, but he didn't feel like he could stop there. He pictured Gunderson showing up to find Tony passed out. Tony took his second shower of the day and tried to calm his mind, but it wasn't working. The faceless smile was no longer just in his nightmares. Tony could see it everywhere now, could sense it staring at him and hear it laughing. Tony was sure he wouldn't last much longer without descending into madness.

Tony tried to think of only happy thoughts. He focused as hard as he could on only thinking about his days at Northwestern, the early years with Katherine and Angelique's smile. He somehow managed to maintain his sanity until Gunderson arrived.

Tony greeted Gunderson at the door and welcomed him into his hotel room. Gunderson noticed the half-bottle of Macallan.

"You have fine taste in scotch, I see," Gunderson said with a cordial smile. "Do you mind if I have a glass?"

"Not at all," Tony replied. "Help yourself, Mr. Gunderson."

"Thank you. And please, call me Bill," Gunderson said. "May I pour you a glass as well?"

"Yes, I could use one about now."

Gunderson poured two glasses of scotch, handed one to Tony and the two sat down. Gunderson set the bottle between them so they wouldn't have to get up to pour a second glass.

"So, Bill," Tony said, "what is it about my case that would bring you here to my room? You haven't worked a case in quite a while as I understand it."

"You're right, I haven't," Gunderson replied. "But you have probably heard whispers about my political aspirations. Maybe I just miss the rush of a trial. Perhaps I just need to win one more case before I completely leave the legal profession. And maybe I just hate the idea of an innocent man being condemned for something he didn't do."

"What makes you think I'm innocent? I'm pretty sure my

own attorney doesn't think I'm innocent. He repeatedly says he does, but I think he just keeps lying to himself, hoping that he will eventually believe it. Either that, or he says it so that if he wins he won't feel guilty for letting a monster go free."

"I hate to tell you this, Mr. Michaels, but you chose poorly. Mr. Wood has never worked a case of this magnitude. Sure, he was worked with many members of the Cowboys, so he is used to the celebrity, but those have mostly been minor charges that he was able to handle with little difficulty and little attention."

"So you would have taken this case in a different direction? And please, call me Tony."

"I'm sure you have done your research on me, Tony. You're most likely aware that I was formerly a prosecutor. I worked closely with the police and the crime lab to ensure that I could get convictions. I know how they think. I know what they look for, and I know how they interpret things.

"As you know," Gunderson continued, "I have also worked for the defense. Having been on both sides of the judicial system, I believe, gives me a unique perspective. Sure, we fight over what evidence is or isn't admissible in court, but in the end, both sides make their arguments based on the exact same evidence. It all about interpretation, and I believe that from my experience I know how jurors think."

"So what do the jurors think?" Tony asked.

"The fact that they are still deliberating, I think, means they like you and WANT to believe you. But I think as the evidence was presented they will ultimately have no choice but to convict you. Which is unfortunate, because I'm confident that you are innocent."

Gunderson had finished his scotch as had Tony. Gunderson filled both glasses once again.

"I appreciate the confidence, but I'm still not sure why you would think that."

"Tony, your house was surprisingly clean, yet showed very little signs of the kind of cleanup that this would have required. There was no chemical smell in the house. The crime scenes I have visited where the perpetrator tried to clean up tend to stink of cleaning products days later. Your wife and son were brutally dismembered, but there was virtually no sign of blood.

"Even if you had killed them," Gunderson said, "I don't think you would have been able to pull off such a massive cleanup. The evidence tells me that somebody else took your wife and child to another location, then brought them back, placed their bodies in your backyard, and planted the little bit of blood that was found. Whoever did it probably planted the blood on your partially burned sweatshirt after the fire went out to make it look as though you were just sloppy in cleanup."

"That's quite a story," Tony said. "It could be exactly what happened, because I know I didn't do it. I'm curious what makes you think that. And why wouldn't the police have considered it?"

"Like I said, Tony, years of experience. It's possible the police considered it, but with no evidence to back that up, it was much easier to convict you than to chase a ghost. In a high-profile case, the public demands that somebody pay, especially when children or pregnant women are involved. To the police, you HAD to be guilty. It would have been very inconvenient if you weren't, especially with no leads to go on in terms of other suspects."

Tony's head was spinning.

"So if you were to take my appeal, how confident are you that we could win and get a conviction overturned."

"One hundred percent. There's no doubt in my mind," Gunderson replied. "The question is whether you would be willing to hire me."

"Why WOULDN'T I hire you?" Tony asked, amazed that it was even a question. "You just made a better case for me in the last few minutes than my lawyer made during the whole trial."

"Well, Tony, here's where it gets interesting," Gunderson said as he got up, walked to the window and paused for a moment. When he walked back he noticed Tony's eyes had followed him, but not his head. Gunderson smiled.

"The reason I am so confident we would win is because I know you can't possibly be guilty. I know THAT because I am the one who killed your wife and child."

"FUCK YOU!" Tony shouted.

Suddenly there was a face to go with the smile that had haunted Tony every day and night since the murders. Tony was filled with rage. He wanted to leap at Gunderson and rip him apart. Tony was going to kill him—right here, right now.

But nothing happened. Tony's brain told his body to attack, but his body didn't respond.

"What the hell?"

"Now, Tony, I need you to remain calm, because there is nothing you can do here. Only a handful of people know this, but after I finished my military duty I was recruited by the CIA. I chose to go to law school, but I did somewhat of, shall we say, an 'internship' with the agency. When I graduated I moved to Baltimore, partly to be close to the Capitol, hoping to gain some powerful friends, and partly to be close to Langley. Let's simplify it to say I have done some 'consulting' for them. One of the perks of that consulting is I get some toys.

"What I put in your scotch is one of my favorites," Gunderson said, smiling the smile from all of Tony's nightmares. "You will be paralyzed until morning. Within an hour you will be asleep and when you wake up you will have no recollection of this, and there will be no traces of anything in your bloodstream.

"So the important question here, Tony, is this: Can you make a deal with the devil? I need to know the answer as you have a short period of time left before you lose the ability to speak. If you agree to let me defend you at your appeal, I can guarantee your freedom.

"You will have forgotten this conversation," Gunderson continued, "but deep down in the dark corner of the basement of your brain which you won't be able to access, you will know that the man who earned that freedom for you is the same man who sliced your wife and child apart while they were still alive. But it's that or the needle for you. You can't win an appeal without me. You can't lose with me. Simple choice here, really.

"If you will agree now, I will start working on your case right away," Gunderson added. "I'll meet with you again tomorrow and go through some paperwork and questions. You won't remember any of this, so you will just think you hired me because I am a better lawyer. But right now you know the truth, so can you live your life in freedom, knowing what you know right now?"

"GO TO HELL!!" Tony spat the words out with contempt and rage.

"Well, I am sure they have a spot reserved for me there, perhaps even a job," said Gunderson proudly.

"Why did you kill them?" Tony asked. "Why would you tell me, you sadistic piece of shit?"

"That's an easy answer," Gunderson said as he poured himself another glass of scotch. "This is my favorite game, and I am very good at it. I hadn't played in a while, and I get bored when I don't get to play. Once I become governor, it will be so much more difficult to play. And I imagine as president, it will be nearly impossible.

"You see, Tony, while I was a prosecutor I became bored. Getting guilty people convicted is rather easy as long as you are thorough in your job. I was making good contacts at Washington and Langley, but I needed more excitement. I needed more of a challenge. So I reflected on my life and what I really wanted to do.

"It occurred to me that what I really missed was killing people, watching their life slip away. It used to give me an erection when I was a sniper. But after a while, shooting people from hundreds of yards away gets less satisfying the more you do it. I wanted to be closer and to feel the life leaving their bodies. I also wanted to punish people who deserved to be punished.

"It gave me a new way to challenge myself. Could I do it in a way that I could get away with it and manipulate the evidence so somebody of my choosing was punished for the murders? Unfortunately, I didn't get to prosecute every one of the cases, but there was an amazing satisfaction in doing my job so well that I could prosecute a man I knew deserved punishment for other things, but was innocent of the charges against him. I think I liked that part even better than the actual killing.

"Like I said before, it had been too long since I played my game, and it may become increasingly difficult for me to play in the near future. I needed one last game.

"I chose you the first time I saw your billboard. I followed you often. I was at Hooters the first time you cheated on your wife. The billboards began to make me laugh. I knew about your fight over moving to New York. I knew about Angelique, such a lovely girl. It's a shame she had to go through this. I knew you were going to leave your pregnant wife. There was plenty of motive.

"I also chose you for symbolic reasons. The people of your ilk are so quick to condemn others. As soon as somebody is questioned for a crime, the media is quick to convict them. You poison the minds of jurors long before the courts are ready to select the jury. You play judge. You play jury. You play God from your chair at the news desk. You look down your nose at others. 'The Most Trusted Man in Texas'? That's quite a punch line.

"To be honest, I was curious how your media brethren would treat you. I wasn't sure if they would be nicer to you than most or be more brutal than usual. I thought it would be fun to chum the water a little bit and see what happened. It was quite entertaining. They turned on you quite quickly. I would have come up with something more exciting than the 'Anchor of Death' myself, but I wasn't consulted on that. Watching this trial and all the media coverage was the most fun I have had in years. CNN even *paid* me for my wonderful insight."

"Fuck you," Tony said again. "I'll tell everyone about this, and you will get the needle, not me."

"I thought you were smarter than that, Tony, tsk, tsk, tsk!" said Gunderson shaking his head. "Did you forget the part where you won't remember this in the morning? Even if you could remember, who would believe you? With all of the charity work I do, nobody would *want* to believe you. You could ask every Texan alive and you won't find anyone who will say I have so much as even farted in church. Any accusations you might make against me will be dismissed as the mad ramblings of a homicidal psychopath who murdered his family and is desperately spouting nonsense hoping to avoid paying for his transgressions.

"Even if you remembered every word of this conversation, who would believe you that I came to your room and confessed to you? If somebody confessed to me that he murdered my wife, I would probably kill him on the spot. You didn't try to harm me at all or even call the police. All I would have to say is that I came to your room because you wanted to discuss your case. I chose not to pursue it, and you are merely lashing out because I would not to take your case. The security footage from the hotel will show me walking in calmly and walking out calmly. Who would ever believe such a ridiculous story? But like I said, you won't remember, so while you are still awake, don't waste your time on such futile thoughts.

"Be honest with yourself about this. I have many powerful friends. I can guarantee your freedom. You can run off with that hot little mistress of yours and do whatever you want. You'll have plenty of money left over to start anew. You just have to let me represent you."

"Kiss my ass," Tony said.

"If that's really the way you want it. As long as I'm here, I'd love to show you something."

Gunderson poured the last of the scotch into his glass. He pulled out his tablet and began showing Tony pictures from the night of the murder. As he flipped through the pictures, he told Tony how he managed the whole thing.

"You see, one night when I followed you home from Hooters, you were drunk and forgot to close your garage door. I walked in and placed a tiny camera in your house so I could get your security code in case I ever needed it. While I was in the house, I stole one of your spare keys. On the way out I noticed the saw in your garage and bought the exact same model.

"Once I had your key and security code, I didn't have to worry about access; it was simply a matter of timing. While you were at Hooters the night your family died, I went to your house and gave your wife and son what I gave you to-night, but with a stimulant rather than a sedative. They were not sleeping when you got home. They were wide awake, just paralyzed. Since I no longer needed the camera I took it so the police wouldn't find it. I thought about leaving it so I could watch, but why take that risk? Then I sat and waited for you to get home.

"Look, there you are," Gunderson smiled as he showed Tony a picture of himself lying on the bedroom floor passed out. "You were out cold. It took some effort getting your clothes off and getting you into bed. I even cleaned up your puke for you. I would think you would be more grateful. I wouldn't even do that with my own vomit. I would make the maid do it for me. I figured you were plenty drunk enough, but I gave you a little sedative to make sure you wouldn't wake up to realize what was happening. Just to be safe.

"I threw all you clothes in the fire, but I pulled the sweatshirt out and let the rest burn off. Look, there's your wife. She was a beautiful woman, Tony, why would you ever cheat on her? I stabbed your wife in the abdomen first. You clearly didn't want that baby anyway. They were both wide awake as I cut them. I cut your son first. I sat your wife in a chair so she could watch. Cute kid. I let him bleed out and die quickly. Children are too precious. I didn't want him to suffer. Then I cut your wife up, threw some blood on your sweatshirt and grabbed a syringe full of blood. I think she may have gone into cardiac arrest before I could finish cutting her which is too bad.

"I took them back to your house, stacked them up by the firewood, planted the sweatshirt and the blood on your ring, replaced your clean blade with my bloody blade, then wiped down everything in your garage. No real reason. I was just curious what the police would think of that. I mean, any experienced killer would be wearing gloves and not leave prints, and there's no reason for a man to wipe prints off things in his own home.

"I really didn't expect things to happen so quickly. I thought you would make it home. I wondered if you would notice the sweatshirt. I was really curious to see your reaction. I'm disappointed I was cheated out of that. I was also curious to see how long you would wait before reporting them missing. The police never found my camera that I had focused on the bodies. I thought maybe with a winter storm approaching you would want to build a fire and I wanted to see your reaction if you were the one who found them.

"I was a little disappointed by that, and it's a shame about the neighbor boy. I wonder how badly this will scar him. Seeing you punch the police officer was fun though. I did enjoy that. I'm not sure it made up for not seeing your reaction to the sweatshirt or the bodies, but it was still fun for me.

"I'm really surprised the police or your lawyers weren't able to figure that all out. It really is a shame. Except for cheating on your wife, you seem like a nice guy. You were one heck of a quarterback too.

"One thing I have never been able to do though, is confess what I had done. Since this is potentially my last game, I had to tell you or I might not get another chance. I was really hoping you would have called my office first, rather than Mr. Wood. It would have been a much cleaner and much easier process for you. By now, you would have been acquitted. But you made the wrong decision. That's why I offered to take your appeal. I have enough connections I could have sped up the process considerably.

"It didn't have to be this way, Tony. I wanted us to be friends and to see you to walk free. I truly did. I would have even offered you a job on my campaign, put you in charge of media relations. I'm sorry we couldn't come to an agreement. I can see you are getting tired now. I should go and let you rest. I would help you into bed, but I'm guessing you don't want my help. This was a great talk. I hope you enjoyed the pictures. Good luck in court."

Gunderson calmly walked out of the room. Downstairs he waved to the concierge and gave his ticket to the valet who ran off to get his car. Gunderson smiled. This had been a fun night.

Miss Cook sent Tony a text message Thursday night to check on him. He seemed to be growing more depressed each day and she worried about him. When he didn't respond, she waited and sent another text. When she got no response from that, she called and got no answer so she headed to the hotel.

Miss Cook found Tony passed out in a chair with an empty bottle of scotch next to him. She tried to think if she had seen the bottle before. Did he drink the whole bottle tonight? She tried to rouse him, but no response. She frantically searched the room for any pills or medication, wondering if Tony had tried to kill himself. Tony was breathing shallow, but he was breathing. She was contemplating calling 911 when Tony said something unintelligible. She tried talking to him, but the answers did not come out in actual words.

Miss Cook decided to wait on the 911 call. She tried to get Tony to snap out of it, but he wasn't improving. Tony weighed twice what Miss Cook weighed, but she thought it was best to get him in bed and lying down. She knew CPR and would call 911 if she needed to, but she didn't want to cause too much of a commotion if Tony had just had a little too much to drink. From the trial she knew Tony could consume a lot of alcohol in one sitting and be all right. She hoped he didn't have that much tonight.

Tony wasn't helping, but Miss Cook was tough. She managed to get Tony the few feet from the chair to the bed. She took off his shoes, pants, and shirt and tucked him in. Then sat in the chair next to him to make sure he was okay, her phone at the ready just in case.

Sometime after midnight, Miss Cook noticed that Tony's breathing appeared to be more normal. Eventually, he began to move some, and then turned on his side. Miss Cook decided that Tony would be fine. She waited another hour to be sure, then went home. She didn't want Tony to know she had been there.

While Miss Cook was frantically worrying about Tony's well-being, Gunderson went home and took his wife out to dinner. He was in a great mood and wanted to celebrate. It was too bad, he thought, that he couldn't tell his wife why he was in such a great mood.

Gunderson had been playing this sadistic game of his since before they met. He wasn't even sure how many families he had killed, plus some occasional individuals from time to time. It must have more than a dozen families. He might even be getting close to 100 victims by now, not counting the people he killed in the army or for the CIA. He would have to check on that. It would be a pity if he had reached the century mark without a proper celebration. He couldn't even remember them all, but he decided he should go through his records and add them up.

Gunderson thought his first family murder was a stroke of genius. There was a club volleyball coach in Baltimore accused of molesting several of his young players. Another prosecutor had the case. The coach walked. Gunderson waited to see if one of the fathers might kill the coach out of revenge, thinking that is what he would do if he had a daughter and one of her coaches took advantage of her.

When no fathers took action, Gunderson decided the coach needed to pay for his sins. It would have been simple to just set up his rifle somewhere and gun him down, but that would too merciful. The coach did not deserve to get off so easily. So Gunderson snuck into the house late one night as the coach was taking his trash out to the curb. Gunderson grabbed the coach as he returned to the garage. He forced the coach to drink something his friends at the CIA had given him, and as the coach collapsed, Gunderson gently lowered him to the ground.

Gunderson then went inside the house and slit the throats of the coach's wife and three daughters while they slept. The home had hardwood floors in the dining room. Gunderson pried up several floorboards and laid the bodies under the floor. He cleaned up the bedrooms, then took the cleaning products and bloody sheets downstairs. He placed those with the bodies. He put new linens on the beds and went back to the garage. He carried the coach to his bed and placed the knife in his hands to get the fingerprints.

Then Gunderson placed the knife with the bodies and replaced the floorboards, strategically cracking a couple of them as he did so. The coach woke up the next morning and reported his family missing. The police at first suspected the wife would have run off with the girls to protect them from their predator father. Her car was parked in the garage, so if that was the case she must have had help.

As the police searched the house for evidence one of the floorboards snapped and gave way. The officer fell awkwardly into the hole, breaking his ankle in the process. Another officer rushed to his side and as he helped his comrade, the second officer noticed blood through the hole in the floor. He pulled up the broken wood and saw a hand. He continued pulling up the floor until he had discovered all four bodies, the bloody sheets and the murder weapon.

As luck would have it, Gunderson drew the case as prosecutor. He knew it would be a slam dunk. There was no jury who would let the coach walk for this, especially after the coach had walked on the rape allegations. Gunderson took a lot of satisfaction for that conviction. When other inmates found out who he was, the rapist volleyball coach who murdered his wife and daughters was repeatedly beaten, raped and then finally killed in prison. That, Gunderson thought, was true justice.

Getting a conviction against a guilty man was easy. Getting a conviction against a man he knew to be innocent was more of a challenge. Gunderson studied every case and every trial he could. He tried to get inside the heads of the police officers he worked with as well as the people in the crime lab.

Gunderson became an expert at making the evidence say whatever he wanted. Sometimes it said homicide. Sometimes it said murder/suicide. Gunderson knew how to cover his tracks and be invisible inside homes.

The volleyball coach had given Gunderson a satisfaction he had never felt before. He delighted in the prosecution and in the news of what later happened to the coach. Gunderson believed this was his true calling. It became easier and more enjoyable the more he did it.

But with all the victims Gunderson had murdered or framed over the years, one thing bothered him. He had never had the satisfaction of bragging about his achievements. Sure, Hunter Johnson knew Gunderson killed his wife, but Johnson had hired Gunderson to do the job. Johnson wasn't about to let his wife take billions in a divorce. Gunderson had done some "favors" for a Texas senator who knew Johnson. The senator put the two in touch.

Gunderson promised Johnson the murder would make him look guilty, but he would leave enough problems with the evidence for an easy acquittal. If Johnson was willing to withstand a little heat, his problems would be solved. It was easy to defend Johnson. Since Gunderson was the real killer, he knew the answer to every question, and he knew every question to ask to get his client acquitted.

Yes, Johnson had known, but that was different because Johnson had hired him. Being able to tell Tony Michaels to his face had brought such sheer joy and delight to Gunderson. Showing the pictures to Michaels who had no power to react brought Gunderson the ultimate satisfaction.

Yes, today was a day of days. If Gunderson had to give up his murderous ways to take public office, this was a brilliant way to wrap up this chapter of his life.

As Gunderson had promised, Tony woke up Friday morning with no recollection of the night before. But he had a sense the devil himself had been in his room. He struggled mightily to remember even the slightest detail. He remembered that he had called Gunderson. Everything else was a complete blank. He saw the empty bottle of Scotch and thought maybe he finished it off. That might obscure his memory. He checked his phone and noticed the texts and missed calls from Miss Cook.

Tony called Miss Cook, who didn't want to embarrass Tony or say anything that might concern him. She didn't mention coming to the room, helping him to bed or staying well past the point she was certain Tony was not in danger. She simply said that she was checking in on him because she was concerned over how he was dealing with waiting for the jury. Tony said it was difficult, but he was managing. She said to call if he needed anything. Tony said he would.

Tony decided to have breakfast in his room rather than downstairs so he called in his order. He tried to remember last night but nothing was there. It wasn't the usual alcohol-induced fog where the mind could slowly piece a few things together; it was a completely blank slate. He eventually gave up, figuring it must not have been important. He turned on the television. Since he was avoiding the news, there was little of interest on. He had already watched all the pay-per-view movies so he put on some cartoons and tried to not think about anything at all.

Tony was watching *SpongeBob SquarePants* when there was a knock at his door. It was Miss Cook.

"I've been really worried about you lately," she said. "And I don't want you to be alone right now."

For a split second Tony remembered the long hug, the kiss on the cheek. In a quick flash of imagination, Tony could see Miss Cook letting her hair down for the first time, ripping her blouse open and seducing him. Before Tony could decide how he would react the rational part of his brain assured him that Miss Cook was far too proper and professional to do that.

Tony's next thought was to desperately hope Miss Cook wasn't here to read Bible passages and pray. That would have been more than Tony could handle at the moment. Tony's mind raced through all the other possible reasons Miss Cook could be here and all the possible reactions he could have . . . until he saw Angelique, who was now back to her natural blond.

Tony stood speechless.

"Mr. Wood doesn't know I did this," Miss Cook said. "So please don't get me in trouble for this. But I thought Angelique would help you until we get a verdict. In the meantime, I am praying for you. Good luck and stay strong."

"SpongeBob?" was the first thing Angelique said. "Really???"

Miss Cook quietly slipped out into the hallway, closing the door behind her, leaving the two alone.

Angelique smiled and kissed Tony. He had really missed both the smile and the kiss. They sat on the bed and continued to watch cartoons and talk about anything except the case. They were still watching cartoons when room service brought them lunch. Eventually, they couldn't take any more cartoons. Nothing of quality was on so they watched the movie *Stealth*.

"Do you think Jessica Biel is sexier than me?" Angelique asked.

"No chance," Tony said. "You're much sexier. Not even close."

"Are you sure?" Angelique asked again. "She's pretty hot. I think I would do her."

They both laughed, and they continued to laugh throughout the movie. It warmed Angelique's heart to hear Tony's laughter and see his smile.

Tony got a text from Wood. "Jury says no verdict today. That means somebody is still fighting for you. So try to relax and enjoy the weekend."

"Who was that from?" Angelique asked, feigning jealousy. "Now that you're notorious you probably have women throwing themselves at you."

"No, it was my lawyer," Tony smiled. "No verdict today, so I'm still free through the weekend."

"Free? You're not free," Angelique said, climbing over to straddle Tony and removing her top. "You're my prisoner, and I'm never letting you free."

Tony and Angelique spent the rest of the weekend in bed, talking, laughing and having sex. They only got up to shower and open the door for room service. They managed to get through the entire weekend acting like it was just a vacation, with not a single mention of the trial.

The vacation continued until Monday afternoon when Wood called Tony to let him know the jury reached a verdict. The judge ordered that the verdict be read Tuesday morning at 11 o'clock.

"We have to be serious for a little bit," Tony said. "And figure out what we are going to do after tomorrow."

"Well," Angelique started off her soliloquy, "I think we should just live as freely as possible. No jobs, just life. See everything! Do everything! Let's run with the bulls! Let's go to Rio for Carnival! Let's see the Sphinx! The Great Wall of China! The Great Barrier Reef. Let's swim with dolphins! Swim with sharks. Let's go to Italy, make our own pasta, make our own wine and make love every night until we're exhausted. Let's go to every island where couples like to go on honeymoons. If we find a place that feels like home we can stop, but let's cram as much into life as we possibly can."

Angelique's enthusiasm made Tony smile. But he had to bring her back to reality.

"Sweetie, that sounds awesome," he replied. "I can't think of a better way to live. Or a better person to do that with.

But there is a good chance the verdict is going to come back against me, and we need to plan for that as well."

"What's to plan?" Angelique said. "You aren't guilty so if they get it wrong, you appeal, and you keep appealing and you keep fighting until they get it right. Eventually they will. So you can't give up on me. You can't give up on us. It kills me to see this happening to you, but whoever did this, you can't let them win. I've never given up on you, and you can't give up on yourself. No matter how bad it might get."

Angelique refused to cry. She could see the tears in Tony's eyes, but again, she wouldn't let him see them in hers. The lioness wanted to find out who did this and devour him. She embraced Tony.

"We can't be sad," she said softly. "We have to stay positive and think positive. Yes, we may lose tomorrow. But we will keep fighting until we win. Now let's order some dinner and some alcohol and celebrate the fact that for tonight, you are still a free man."

When court was reconvened, the jury delivered their verdict. Tony was found guilty of all charges. Judge Randall thanked the jury and dismissed them. Sentencing was set for Monday the 18th at which time Tony would be taken into custody. He was to spend the time in between getting all his affairs in order. Fortunately, the house was already sold, so that was one less thing that needed to be done. Really, all Tony needed to do was to write a will and set up an account from which he could pay for his appeals and set some aside for Angelique.

Upon news of his verdict, Tony's mother had a heart attack and died. Tony was allowed to travel to Chicago for the funeral wearing a GPS-tracking bracelet and accompanied by two federal marshals. Angelique also flew to Chicago for the funeral. After the funeral, they embraced.

"You're all I have left," Tony said through tears.

"Then just keep fighting," Angelique said. "You're still mine until the 18th, and I won't stop fighting until I get you back."

The marshals led Tony away. Angelique got a cab to the airport and flew back to Dallas. She didn't want to cry in front of Tony. She had to stay strong in front of him to give him strength. But on the flight, she let it all out, allowing herself one moment of weakness. She spent that night at her apartment crying until she was sure it was all out of her system. Then she packed enough clothes to last until the 18th and headed to Tony's hotel.

Angelique wanted to make her last days with Tony as fun as possible. They played games, told stories and jokes, watched movies and cartoons and enjoyed each other's company. Both had heavy hearts, but both refused to show it. Neither wanted to admit it, but they both knew there was a possibility they would never see each other again.

Neither mentioned the situation until Friday the 15th when Tony finally spoke his mind.

"Angelique," Tony spoke. "I promise to keep fighting, but we both know the reality of the situation. There is a good chance that once I get thrown in prison, I'm never getting out. Even if I win an appeal, it could take years and everything that's left of my money. Katherine and TJ were killed, and I'm going to prison. I don't want your life to be ruined as well. Live life and enjoy it. Don't waste it waiting for me, because

I may never be given the chance to get out. I want you to be happy."

"The only way I will ever be happy is with you," Angelique said. "I want to do all those things I talked about, but if I did them without you or with somebody else, I would feel empty inside. So no more talk about this. The only way I waste my life is by turning my back on you. I'll never do that. I'm going to wait as long as it takes. I fought this hard to get you. I'm not giving up now."

Neither spoke for minutes. Then a lightbulb clicked on for Angelique.

"I was watching CNN one night," she said. "There was this legal expert . . . Gunner-something. He said he thought you were framed. He said Wood wasn't up for the case and a better lawyer would have gotten you acquitted. You should call him."

"What did you just say?"

"I know you told me not to watch the news," Angelique began apologetically. "I almost never did, but one night I had to."

"Not that part, sweetie."

"There was this guy who said you were framed and you're innocent. I said you should call him."

"Bill Gunderson?" Tony said. Angelique nodded. "I did call him."

Angelique got excited thinking Tony might have a chance to win an appeal.

"What did he say?" The life was coming back into Angelique's voice. "Is he going to take your case? Are we going to win?"

"Honestly, I can't remember a thing."

"How can you not remember? I don't get it."

"All I remember is that I called him. I spoke to him on the phone, but I don't remember anything he said. I think he was coming by, but I don't even remember him being here. I don't remember anything from that night. I don't remember seeing him, I don't remember going to bed. I remember my night-mares were worse than usual, but when I woke up, I couldn't remember those either.

"I woke up scared," Tony continued "like something awful had happened. But nothing was wrong with me. I was a mess all day. I thought it was just me panicking about the jury. That was the day you came over. I had forgotten about it until now."

"I hate to sound dumb, but I still don't get it."

"You're not dumb, baby. I don't get it either. Do you know where my phone is?"

"It's by the TV. Are you going to call Gunderson?"

"No," Tony said. "Something isn't adding up. I don't know why but Gunderson is the last person I want to talk to right now. I need to call an old friend. I haven't talked to him in a while. Let's hope he's able to come through for us."

Tony scanned through his contacts and made a call. Angelique crossed her fingers.

"Samuels here," said the voice on the other line.

"Ryan, thank God. It's Tony Michaels. I need a huge favor."

Tony didn't want to give too many details over the phone, but he begged for Samuels to come to the hotel to meet with him.

Ryan Samuels was a former police officer who quit the force and became a private investigator about the same time

Tony was getting his start at Channel 9. Samuels was investigating a local car dealership at the time.

An employee came to him claiming the owner was stealing from employee commissions and scamming customers. The employee tried the police and the manufacturer but hadn't gotten anywhere so he asked Samuels to investigate. Samuels began investigating the dealer and found some evidence suggesting the dealer was indeed corrupt, but not enough to bring the dealer down or make him pay back all the people he had been ripping off. So Samuels contacted Tony to see if he could help him bring his investigation to light.

At the time, Samuels saw Tony as a hungry, ambitious reporter. He thought they could help each other by working together. Tony agreed and spent time reviewing the notes Samuels provided and began working hand in hand with Samuels on the investigation. Once Tony found enough people willing to speak on camera he put a piece together and aired it on Channel 9.

Shortly after the piece aired, a federal investigation was launched on the dealer, who also owned dealerships in Oklahoma and Louisiana. A class action lawsuit was filed on behalf of customers and employees. The dealer was indicted and later found guilty on several counts. He lost the lawsuit as well and lost everything he owned to pay back the damages.

Tony got his first local Emmy in Dallas for that piece, and Samuels gained credibility as a private investigator. The two worked together occasionally after that and developed a friendship. They hadn't spoken much recently, both being too busy with their lives.

Now, Tony saw Samuels as his final hope. Samuels agreed to meet Tony at the hotel for breakfast Saturday morning.

Tony told Samuels the relevant details about his case, insisting he was framed. He then mentioned that Gunderson approached him at the end of the trial about taking his appeal, said something about Tony being found guilty, but Gunderson was sure he was innocent and that he could do a better job than Jake Wood had done.

Tony told Samuels that Gunderson had visited him at the hotel and that he couldn't recall anything much beyond opening the door and letting Gunderson into the room. He told Samuels about the horrific nightmares he had, the feeling of helplessness. He thought he remembered waking up after one of the nightmares, wanting to get a drink of water, but he was unable to move. Maybe that had just been another nightmare, but there was something definitely wrong about the meeting with Gunderson.

"Are you trying to tell me you think Gunderson killed your family?" Samuels asked incredulously. "Bill Gunderson—the guy everybody says is the next governor of Texas if he wants it?"

"I'm not saying he killed them," Tony said. "But something's definitely not right. If he didn't kill them, he at least knows something. I'm begging you to find out what that is. You're my last hope."

"I saw him on CNN," Angelique added. "He said he thought based on the evidence that Tony was framed. He said he thought somebody abducted Katherine and TJ, killed them somewhere else and then brought them back. He sounded very confident about it, but the police and Tony's lawyer never found anything to back that up."

"So you think he would go on national TV to brag about how he killed them and framed Tony?" Samuels asked. "That would take balls the size of Texas. Are you *sure* that's what he said?"

"He didn't say he did it," Angelique replied. "But he was very convinced that Tony was framed. He seemed to know more about the case than anybody else. I want to know everything about this guy. If you'll investigate, I want to help. I'll even try to get a job at his office and snoop around if it will help."

"Whoa, hold your horses there," Samuels said. "If, and I mean this is a very big IF, but *if* Gunderson either did this or knows who did, he's very dangerous. He will recognize you even if we dye your hair and get you a fake ID and Social Security Number. You can help, but I won't let you do anything that will get you hurt or killed."

"So you're in?" Tony asked.

"I've got to help an old friend," Samuels said. "I'm not sure I believe you about Gunderson yet, but I do believe you didn't do this. I can't let you get the needle or rot away in prison. It's not going to be easy, but I'll start digging. I'll keep in touch with Angelique and if there's anything we can use to get you out, we'll use it."

Tony and Angelique both thanked Samuels. They all shook hands.

"Good luck," Tony said.

"You too, my friend," Samuels replied. "You too."

Katherine's family had not shown up at all during the trial. Tony was hoping they would show up for sentencing so he could face them and tell them that he didn't do this. He wanted to admit to being a bad husband, but he wanted them to know Katherine was a wonderful person and he really did care for her. He wanted them to believe he was innocent. He wanted them to know that he was going to keep fighting because he wanted justice for her.

But Katherine's family did not show up for sentencing. They chose not to face the man they had treated like a son, who had been accused and now convicted of taking away their only daughter in such a horrific manner.

The judge gave Tony a chance to speak before he handed down the sentence.

"I didn't do this," Tony said as his voice shook. "I hope to prove that someday. In the meantime, I apologize to Katherine's family. I apologize to Katherine for not being a better husband and a better friend. I apologize to my son for not being a better father. I apologize to Angelique for not finding the answers that could have led to a different verdict. And I apologize to all my friends, neighbors and coworkers who have had to deal with this. I am not by any means an innocent man, but I am innocent of these charges, and I will fight until my last breath to find justice for Katherine and TJ."

Angelique was seething. The lioness scanned the courtroom for Gunderson, wanting to rip his throat open. She decided he was a coward for not showing. The rest of the courtroom was silent.

"Mr. Michaels," Judge Randall said, "a jury of your peers has found you guilty of murdering your wife, your son and your unborn baby. I find the nature of these murders to be especially egregious and heinous. I have no choice but to sentence you to die by lethal injection. You still maintain your innocence, and you will have the opportunity to appeal. But barring a successful appeal you will spend the rest of your days on Death Row at the United States prison in Beaumont.

"Mr. Michaels," Judge Randall continued, "you have appeared to be genuinely full of sorrow over what has happened. Although you have maintained your innocence to the last, this court has found you guilty. I don't think even the Lord will have mercy on somebody who could destroy lives in this manner.

"This court is adjourned," Randall said, his gavel slamming down like a clap of thunder from the heavens.

Angelique thought she would cry. But instead she just watched in anger as Tony was led away in handcuffs toward a bus bound for Beaumont. The lioness was now furious. She would stay that way until she found justice.

Tony's cell was a tiny dark room with no comforts, almost no light. There was a small sink and a hole in the corner for Tony to use as a toilet. Tony was not allowed visitors, and he was only able to leave his cell for a maximum of one hour each day. Meals were slid into his cell through a slot in the door. He was not given utensils. Compared to this, Tony thought the needle seemed appealing. He often thought of giving up, but Angelique wrote to him every day, finishing every letter with "I love you. Stay strong."

When Angelique wasn't writing to Tony, she was working out as hard as she could. She was calling Samuels multiple times daily to see if he had any information or needed her help. She spent the rest of her time trying to research Gunderson online or trying to work with Jake Wood on anything that might help with the appeal. Angelique had allowed herself the brief moment of weakness after the funeral, but she was now growing stronger and more determined each day.

Angelique also sent some blank journals to Tony and

occasionally he would write in them, his thoughts, memories or song lyrics—anything to help fill his day and take his mind outside the walls of the prison, even if only briefly. The letters and the journals were the only thing that kept Tony going in prison.

The nightmares still haunted him, so he tried to remember those last days in the hotel with Angelique as much as possible. He would sometimes sing theme songs from television programs just to keep him distracted from his reality. There was little else to do, except fight to hold on to whatever sanity he had left.

Wood had filed an appeal, but it wouldn't be heard for months. Tony started to calculate the days, hours, minutes left. But he didn't really know how long it would take for a judge to hear his appeal, or how long that appeal would take. Most days he didn't believe the appeal would help. From Tony's perspective, the prosecution's case was weak, but it had definitely been stronger than his. Better to not think about time or the case, he decided.

Occasionally, Tony let himself have hope that his old friend Ryan Samuels would find something. Samuels had been a good cop. Tony found it ironic that he was partners with Detective Thomas while he was on the force. Samuels was a good investigator too. If anybody could get the dirt on Gunderson, it was Samuels.

Back when they were partners, Thomas and Samuels were on patrol a few days before Christmas one year and responded to a call about an armed bank robbery. The suspects led them on a chase to the Dallas Galleria, where they hoped to steal a different car and escape in the holiday shopping crowd.

Thomas and Samuels chased the suspects around the parking lot. In an act of desperation, the suspects crashed through the Nordstrom doors and ran into the mall. Thomas and Samuels called for backup and pursued.

The suspects ran into Victoria's Secret. They demanded that the manager close the gates at the front of the store. When she hesitated, the gunman with brown hair and a goatee shot her in the head. Screams rang out through that end of the mall. The assistant manager agreed to close the gates if they promised not to shoot anybody else.

"I can't promise that," Goatee said. "But I promise I will shoot everyone in here if you don't."

The assistant manager obliged. One of the employees managed to sneak some customers out the back door before being caught and shot in the head as well, this time by the gunman with the long blond hair pulled back into a ponytail. The ponytail gunman took her keys, locked the back door and turned the alarm on.

"If anybody else tries anything funny," Ponytail said, "everybody dies."

Several customers ran to hide in the changing room area. The rest just ducked down, lay on the floor or hid behind anything they could find, praying to make it out of this alive.

Ponytail fired a few shots through the locked gate, hitting a few people in the mall just outside the store. Goatee fired as well, hitting more people as the crowd scattered. Samuels and Thomas got on the radio again, asking where their backup was and demanding it arrive soon. They let them know it was now a hostage situation with gunfire. They were told SWAT was on its way.

With the crowd out front dispersed, Ponytail and Goatee opened fire on the two police officers who were hiding behind the mall directory and a small kiosk. Thomas and Samuels began to return fire. Samuels managed to kill Ponytail with a shot to the head. In desperation, Goatee picked a customer up off the floor and put a gun to her head. Thomas put his hands up and began walking toward the store. When he was sure Goatee could see him, Thomas put his gun on the ground and began talking to him, trying to calm him down.

Thomas was able to keep Goatee talking long enough for the SWAT team to arrive and for a sniper to get a clean shot, killing Goatee and ending the situation. In total, nine innocent people were dead and seven injured. Of the victims, fifteen were shot by the assailants. One of the bullets matched the gun of Officer Samuels. It had ricocheted off the gate and lodged in the spine of a seventeen-year-old girl, who would never walk again.

The investigation concluded that Thomas and Samuels had acted appropriately given the situation. Both were reinstated, but Samuels couldn't go back. He turned in his badge and became a private investigator.

Occasionally, Thomas would call his old partner when he needed some help with an investigation that might involve something beyond the scope of police protocol. Samuels always appreciated the chance to help out his old partner and help put away the bad guys. And it was much more fulfilling than the assignments of following cheating spouses.

It had been awhile since they had worked together, but when Samuels called, Thomas dropped what he was doing and went to meet his old partner immediately.

Samuels met Thomas at a diner they used to frequent in their days as partners.

"Man, it's been too long," Thomas said.

"Definitely," Samuels nodded. "Definitely."

"So why'd you call me out here?" Thomas asked "I know the breakfast is good here, but you didn't invite me just to have some Eggs Benedict."

"You were the lead detective on the Michaels case, right?"

"Yeah, why?"

"Was there anything you found strange or unusual about the case? Maybe things that just didn't add up."

"A few things. To this day I still question whether an innocent man is going to die. But the evidence was strong enough to convict him, and the jury decided he was guilty."

"Did you ever think it was possible Michaels was set up?"

"Like I said, everything was there to convict him, but the pieces just never fit together right. Everything we had pointed to him. My instincts as a cop said it was wrong. They all claim to be innocent, but this guy actually had me believing."

"Did you just give up?"

"No, man, I kept looking for something," said Thomas, shaking his head. "Just for peace of mind. But I couldn't find anything to back him up. Why all the interest in Michaels?"

"Michaels called me before his sentencing and had some unusual things to say," Samuels responded. "This was not typical stuff you would expect from a guy facing a death sentence. He said Bill Gunderson approached him at the trial and said something about wanting to take his appeal because he knew he was innocent. He told me Gunderson came to meet him a few days later but he can't remember anything about the meeting."

"You're shitting me, right?" Thomas laughed. "Bill Gunderson? That man is going to be the next governor. Why would he jeopardize that to kill a news anchor's family?"

"That part I can't figure out either," Samuels said. "But I have been doing some digging. Two months before the murder, Gunderson bought a foreclosed property in the same subdivision, just a couple blocks away from Tony's house. He didn't start any renovation until after the murders, then eventually flipped the house for a six-figure profit. He could have used that house to actually do the killing. Maybe that's why you couldn't find more evidence at the Michaels house."

"So somehow he sneaks in, abducts the wife and kid, takes them to this other house, chops them up and brings them back?"

"It's possible," Samuels suggested. "All the focus was elsewhere. He would have had plenty of time to destroy the evidence if it was somewhere nobody would think to look."

"It is," Thomas agreed. "But it's also possible that's just a coincidence. He may have just made a sound investment. And there are a couple of problems even if you're sure that's the case. For one, you'll never get a warrant in this town for Bill Gunderson. Besides, if there was any evidence in the house, I'm sure Gunderson made sure it was taken care of by the construction crew. You'll also never get a warrant to go in and tear up the new family's house."

"You're right," Samuels conceded. "But I just want you to keep that in the back of your mind. There's more."

"Do tell."

"Before he became a defense attorney, Gunderson was a prosecutor and a damn good one," Samuels said. "He prosecuted four murder cases in that time. All four were fathers accused of killing their families. All four fathers called the police to file a missing persons report. None of the four had alibis but insisted all along on their innocence."

"Don't they all?" Thomas inquired.

"Usually," Samuels acknowledged. "But these guys were pretty adamant. And here's the kicker—all of the bodies were found on family property. The first one, they were under the floor. The second one was an avid hunter, and they found his family in the freezers in the garage under several pounds of venison. The third one had a lake house where he liked to go fishing. The bodies were found there. The fourth one, the bodies were in the attic. Sound familiar?"

"Very familiar," Thomas said thoughtfully.

"If you killed your family, you probably wouldn't hide them in your home. You would most likely dump them in a lake or bury them somewhere nobody would ever look, right?" Samuels continued. "And if they were in your house, you certainly wouldn't call the police and invite them over to snoop around for clues, would you?"

"No," said Thomas. "Michaels never called the cops though."

"He never had the chance," Samuels said. "If you believe his story, they were asleep when he got home. It's not unusual for a wife to take her son out in the morning/early afternoon. No reason for Michaels to panic then. And he never had the chance to get home."

"So if Gunderson did it, he put the bodies outside figuring Michaels would come home, and then panic," Thomas said. "Michaels would call her cell, which she wouldn't answer. So Michaels would call the police. If it was just his wife, we wouldn't have done anything at the time. A missing child though and we would have put out an Amber alert immediately and been right over to look for clues and get a toothbrush or something for a DNA sample."

"Exactly!" exclaimed Samuels. "But the neighbor kids sped up the time line. Want to know something else about Gunderson?"

"Sure."

"Remember the Hunter Johnson case?"

"Yeah, big shot oil and cattle tycoon," Thomas said. "Wife caught him cheating and wanted a divorce. Was going to take billions. Then she had an 'accident.' I remember."

"Johnson was acquitted," Samuels said. "Gunderson was his lawyer. He got about a million in legal fees for the case, which doesn't seem too crazy. But Johnson got cancer and died a few years ago. In his will he gave billions to charities and universities, but he left five billion dollars to Gunderson. That's when Gunderson stopped taking trials and became more of a political figure."

"So it's possible then that the Michaels family is at least the sixth family Gunderson has killed," Thomas said. "But with all that money and a political career on the horizon, why risk it now? And why reveal himself to Michaels? I don't get it."

"He might have just missed killing," Samuels suggested. "He's good at it. It was an itch that he hadn't scratched in a while. Maybe there have been others we don't know about. Maybe he never stopped doing it or maybe it's been too long and he started jonesing for a fix. As for revealing himself to Michaels, that's just arrogance. Gunderson is definitely a narcissist. This whole thing has probably been fun for him."

"You are still one hell of a cop," Thomas said. "I miss having you as a partner. But you know I'd probably lose my badge if I go after Gunderson, and it's going to be almost impossible to pin any of this on him."

"Don't go after him," Samuels said. "If I get anything, I'll come to you. Like I said, just keep it in the back of your mind. Hopefully I can find something before Michaels gets the needle. I'm off to Virginia in the morning."

"Why Virginia?"

"Of the four murderers Gunderson personally convicted, two were executed and one was killed in prison," Samuels said grimly. "Only the fisherman is still alive. He's at the U.S. penitentiary in Virginia. I'm going to go talk fishing with him. Maybe learn something about bait. Might be a wasted trip, but it's worth a shot."

"Can't hurt," Thomas said. "Need me to do anything here?"

"Don't do anything that might get you in trouble," Samuels said. "Gunderson is a powerful figure, and if he's capable of this, he's pretty dangerous. I'm sure he has some pretty powerful friends. If you do anything, be careful. And watch your ass."

"You do the same, my friend," Thomas said.

Upon his arrival in Virginia, Samuels checked into his hotel and reviewed the files on the case of Manny Ortiz, the fisherman. Ortiz was the only survivor left of the murderers that Gunderson had prosecuted. After initially claiming his innocence, Ortiz confessed to the murders and instead of the death penalty received four consecutive life sentences.

Ortiz knew he would never see the outside again and wasn't

sure he wanted to after so many years behind bars. He was allowed visitors, but had not had a single visitor since he went to prison. The letter from Samuels was the first one he had received.

In the letter, Samuels explained that he had a friend in a similar situation as Ortiz. Samuels mentioned he found some other cases with surprising similarities and was hoping to piece them together and find the man who had wrongly put so many people behind bars. Ortiz agreed to speak to Samuels, not so much because he believed Samuels could help him, or because he believed he could help Samuels. Ortiz simply wanted to have a visitor. But if it helped get the guy who set him up, that would be a bonus.

Samuels introduced himself and asked Ortiz to tell his version of the story.

"Well, I had planned a fishing trip with some friends up at my lake house," Ortiz explained. "For one reason or another, they all canceled, but I decided I needed a few days away and that I would go by myself. When I went fishing, I would leave at 2 in the morning so I packed the car the night before. I slept in the spare bedroom and tried to not wake anybody on the way out. I never even bothered to check on my family because I didn't want to disturb them.

"I drove out to the lake," Ortiz continued. "Caught a lot of fish. Threw most of them back, kept enough to feed myself and a couple to bring back home. I had some beers. I just tried to relax. It was good to get away."

"I hear that," Samuels said, nodding. "What happened after that?"

"I went home on Sunday and nobody was there," Ortiz answered. "My wife, Veronica, my two boys, Pedro and

Ramon, and my daughter, little Christina. Nobody was there. I thought maybe they went shopping or to a movie so I waited. I started cooking up some fish and had a couple of beers. I fell asleep watching television. I woke up later and still nobody. So I called the police.

"They came out to the house, talked to me for a little bit, then asked me to go to the station for a statement while they searched the house for any clues. I told them my story, and I was about to leave. They said I should get a hotel while they were still looking at the house. Then they told me I couldn't leave and they started acting like I was guilty.

"They said they found blood at the house and that it had been cleaned up. They said they found hair and blood in some duffel bags in the garage and in the car. They made me give them the address to the lake house and police there found the bodies. Autopsies said they had been killed Thursday night. Can you believe that? Somebody comes into my house and kills my family while I sleep, then follows me to the lake and buries the bodies right next to the lake house?"

"It's quite a story," Samuels said. "But it sounds like a familiar story to me. It might be the same guy who killed my friend's family and set him up."

"So you believe me?" Ortiz asked.

"I think I do."

"Well, congratulations. You're the first one. Not even my own lawyer believed me. I never stood a chance. My family and friends abandoned me. That's why I never bothered to fight."

"Did you have any enemies? Can you think of anybody who would have reason to set you up?" Samuels asked.

"I was a lobbyist, so on any given day, there were plenty of people who didn't like me," Ortiz said. "But as far as I knew, it was all professional. Nobody ever threatened me. I never felt I had any enemies. I spent the first few years in here just trying to think of anybody I had ever met who might want to do this. Never thought of anybody, so I quit worrying about it. I've accepted that I am going to die here. These days I mostly just read books, including the Bible, every day. I figure I should try to get myself right with the Lord. I've been punished enough."

"Was there anything strange about your trial?"

"There was no trial. I made a deal to avoid the death penalty."

"If you were innocent, why not fight? Why confess to something you didn't do?"

"I doubt you can understand this, but I lost everything that was important to me that night," Ortiz said. "When they arrested me, I couldn't afford bail and not a single friend or family member was willing to bail me out. So I sat in jail, and I got raped. I got beaten. My spirit was broken. There was nothing left for me to go back to in the real world. My friends and family let me get raped and beaten. How was I going to ever trust anyone again?

"At the pretrial hearing, something about the lawyer prosecuting the case was strange," Ortiz continued. "Maybe he was trying to impress somebody, but he really wanted me to go down for this. I mean, every lawyer wants to win every case, but it felt like he had something personal at stake. I can't really explain it. And maybe he has one of those photographic memories, but he seemed to know everything about me and my family, and he seemed to know my house better than I knew it."

"So what finally made you confess?" Samuels asked.

"I didn't want to face that lawyer," Ortiz said. "And I didn't want to sit there listening to him describe how my family was murdered and blame me for it. I didn't want to relive the pain of losing my family. If I fought it, I was going to lose anyway. I couldn't afford a real lawyer, and the public defender they gave me told me I had no case. I had nobody in my corner, nothing to keep me going and nothing to look forward to, if, by some miracle, I was freed. I thought the Lord must have been punishing me for something else I've done wrong. So I decided to just not fight it. I confessed before it could get to trial. I didn't think they would take the deal, but they did. Since then, I shut my mouth and I read the Bible every day."

"Thank you, Mr. Ortiz, you've been very helpful."

"You sure you don't want to stay a while?" Ortiz said. "You're the first visitor I've ever had in here. Maybe we can talk some fishing? Or baseball?"

"I really do need to get back to Texas," Samuels said. "But I will keep in touch. I promise."

Back in Texas, Samuels met again with Thomas.

"So what did your fisherman have to say?" Thomas asked.

"If his story didn't sound almost the same as Tony's story and almost the same as those other cases look, I would have never believed him," Samuels said. "He was very convincing about his innocence, but he confessed to the crimes just to avoid the death penalty. He said Gunderson was taking the case very personally, like he had something at stake. He said it struck him as odd how much Gunderson knew about his house and family."

"Maybe Gunderson was just very thorough," Thomas

cautioned. "To play devil's advocate, Gunderson was top of his class at West Point. You don't do that by leaving things to chance. Maybe he took on all his cases the same as he took on his military assignments. Maybe he never left that soldier mentality behind. Maybe he took on every case assuming the other side wasn't just his adversary but his enemy."

"I hear what you're saying, but it's really starting to look like a duck and sound like a duck. I'm going to keep digging."

"Just be careful. Don't be doing anything where I have to arrest you. And don't be doing anything that's going to get my ass in trouble. And if you are right, that means your duck has killed an awful lot of people. Don't be next."

"I'll watch my back, but I have to keep looking."

Two days later Samuels received a call from the warden at the U.S. penitentiary in Pennington Gap, Virginia, to let him know that Manny Ortiz was dead. A fight broke out during lunch and during the skirmish Ortiz was shanked. He died later that day in the infirmary.

The warden called Samuels because he was the only person who had ever visited or written Ortiz. Before he died, Ortiz had requested that Samuels receive his Bible. The warden also said Ortiz had been a model prisoner, was probably the friendliest person at USP Lee and had no enemies.

Samuels was thrown for a loop. Could this be a coincidence? If not, does Gunderson really have that kind of influence and pay so much attention to somebody he put away twenty years ago? If so, Samuels would really have to stay on his toes. But there was no way he could let Gunderson gain political office. Had Gunderson let Ortiz live just because he kept his mouth shut and didn't fight? Was Samuels the reason

Ortiz was now dead? If so, that meant Samuels was probably next.

Samuels was suddenly glad he never married. As a police officer, he was married to the badge and didn't have time for a relationship. After leaving the force, he went through a period of heavy drinking and was difficult to be around. Eventually he just accepted that he was a loner. It helped in his job as a private investigator to not have anybody nagging about his hours or where he had been or what he smelled like.

Now he was just glad that Gunderson didn't have any additional targets. If Gunderson wanted to hurt Samuels, he had to come after Samuels himself. Samuels vowed to be prepared when that happened and was glad he didn't have to worry about protecting anybody else.

Samuels was sitting in his car outside his favorite coffee shop, contemplating all the layers of this case. What had he gotten himself into? He called Thomas to let him know about Ortiz.

"They got to my guy," Samuels said. "They shanked him after I left."

"Hey, it's prison, man," Thomas responded. "These things happen. Prisoners getting shanked is part of that life."

"You don't understand," Samuels said. "The warden described him as the friendliest person in the prison. He had no enemies. Ortiz had accepted his fate. He had accepted that he was going to die in prison and his only goal was to get right with the Lord. People get shanked in prison, but not people like Ortiz."

"So Gunderson has been watching this guy all these years?" Thomas questioned. "He's got somebody on the inside, either a prisoner or guard who tips him off about your visit and he orders a hit? You need a vacation. I think you're going crazy here."

"Ortiz was the only loose end," Samuels said. "Of all the people we know about, everyone else is dead. He was very vocal about his innocence when he was arrested, but suddenly he confessed. His family and friends disowned him. He has no incidents with anybody in prison until he gets his first visitor after twenty years. I ask him some questions about his case and about Gunderson and he gets killed just a couple of days later. Come on, you know that's not a coincidence."

"If he was worried about Ortiz being a loose end, why did he wait so long?" Thomas asked.

"Because Ortiz hadn't given him anything to worry about," Samuels said. "He confessed. He never had a visitor— until me. Nobody wrote to him until me, and he never wrote to anyone. He was going to keep his mouth shut, live the best life he could on the inside and die quietly in prison . . . until I came and stirred the pot."

"Then you had best be watching your back," Thomas replied. "I think you should back off before you get yourself killed. I don't think you can prove this, and you know what he's capable of doing. If he knows about Ortiz, he knows about you. Maybe you should take Angelique on a little vacation. Get your head straight and find somewhere for her to hide out until this is all over with."

"Fred," Samuels said, "when we were partners, how many times did a captain or chief tell us to back off an investigation, and how many of those times did we listen?"

"A lot. And never," Thomas said. "I got your back as much as I can without getting my ass killed or in trouble over this. But I can't say this enough—be careful."

Samuels hung up. He was getting ready to leave when a homeless man approached his car. He slammed a note against the driver's side window.

"HE KNOWS WHEN YOU'VE BEEN BAD OR GOOD, SO BE GOOD FOR GOODNESS SAKE!"

Samuels knew it was both a warning to back off and at the same time was mocking him for the Christmas shooting at the Galleria. The homeless man stepped back and lit the note on fire. It was gone by the time Samuels could get out of the car to confront the man. Samuels grabbed the man by the shirt and slammed him against the car.

"Who gave you that note?"

"Never seen him before in my life," the homeless man said. "I was lying in that alley over there when some guy walks up to me. Says if I put the note in your face and burn it he'll give me a hundred dollars. Says if I don't he's going to kill my dog. My dog Alexis, she's the only thing I got in this world, and I ain't never had a hundred dollars."

"What did he look like? Did he say anything else?"

"I couldn't see his face. Too many shadows, and I was mostly looking at his knife. He said you would understand the message."

"Get out of here," Samuels said with disgust. "And take a damn shower."

Samuels screamed to the sky, wishing he had something to kick or throw. This was personal now. One way or the other, Samuels was going to see this to the end. He just hoped it wouldn't be his own end.

Samuels went to see Simon Gerrard, a hacker he and Thomas once arrested. While Simon was a freshman in high school, he hacked into the American Airlines Center during a Dallas Mavericks game. It was March 14, or as some people like to say, National Pi Day. Simon replaced all the electronic advertisements with pictures of different kinds of pies. He changed the scoreboard to read Mavericks 3.14, Spurs 3.14. All the clocks in the arena read 3:14. The video board alternated between the Pi symbol and pictures of pies. Eventually he returned the clocks and scoreboard to normal so the game could resume, but he left the pie images.

After that stunt, Simon was forever known in the hacker world as the Pieman.

Simon was advanced enough as a hacker to pull this off, but at such a young age he was not advanced enough to not leave a trace. Samuels and Thomas were the officers sent to arrest him. Arena management wanted Simon charged for his prank. The Mavericks owner wanted the charges dropped if Simon would work for him to protect both the team and the arena from future attacks.

Simon had never meant any harm. He was just having some fun and seeing if his skills were good enough to make the prank happen. Simon agreed to the owner's conditions and spent the next several years working for the Mavericks and their owner on various business ventures. He also decided that he wanted to remain on the right side of the law, so he occasionally worked with local law enforcement on cases.

Eventually, Simon decided to freelance his skills. He bought a large home in ritzy Highland Park. He alternately referred to the house as his fortress, lair or bunker. Simon decided the existing home security system was not up to par, so he began working on developing his own system. When he finished he showed it off to his former boss with the Mavericks, who was so impressed he not only wanted Simon to upgrade his personal home security system but start a company to sell the system to high-end homes.

Samuels, who according to Simon, had the same technical knowledge as a goldfish, used Simon quite often with help on his investigations. Simon had more than 100 computers in his home. He turned the master bedroom into his hub, which he referred to as The Bakery. That was where he spent most of his time.

Simon used the smallest room for his bedroom and set up the other rooms with the biggest televisions he could find. Simon never actually watched television. He would occasionally stream movies, but he set each room up for his various gaming systems and furnished them with nothing but Lovesacs and surround sound. If Simon wasn't working, he was playing video games.

The only wall in his house that wasn't covered with a television, a computer monitor or a security monitor was a wall in the living room. For that wall, Simon paid someone to paint a giant mural of his Mavericks prank, complete with players and referees looking up in shock at the scoreboard.

Simon greeted Samuels at the door and invited him into The Bakery. Samuels explained that he needed to get into Gunderson's computer to see if there was anything to link him to the Michaels murders.

"Cool, a murder investigation," Simon said. "Way more interesting than the stuff you usually bring me. It will cost you something extra."

"Trust me, if we get this guy I will take care of you."

Simon got excited when he saw what he was up against. He began explaining the expertise he found in Gunderson's computer and how he would overcome it, but as far as Samuels was concerned, Simon could have been speaking Swahili.

"Slow down, Pieman."

"Right, I forgot I was talking to Fred Flintstone. So your guy either really knows his way around a computer or he pays somebody well to protect him. His hard drive has several partitions and everything has pretty advanced encryption, firewalls and more things that you won't be able to understand.

"Picture it this way: You're in a jungle filled with land mines, trip wires and highly venomous snakes. If you make it through that, at the edge of the jungle there are pygmies in trees with poisoned blow darts. If you make it through that, there are some hungry lions and some angry poachers who don't like you. Thank you for bringing me such a worthy adversary. This will be so much fun! This will take some time, but I will have your pies. Be patient."

Samuels went home and tried to lay as low as possible. He made no phone calls except to check on Angelique. He used a burner phone for that. He was constantly looking out his windows. When he slept, he slept with his shotgun next to him and his pistol under the pillow. When he left the house, he checked under his hood and under the car. He didn't really expect a car bomb, and he wasn't overly concerned about being taken out by a long-range sniper rifle, but he was always on the alert. Samuels was sure Gunderson liked to make his killings personal. He was certain if Gunderson came after him, it would be to his face, and he would be made to suffer. But he couldn't be too careful.

A few days later he got a text from Simon.

"I have your first pie!" Since he had become the Pieman, he wanted everything referred to as pies. If you were callous enough to say "info" or anything generic, you were subjected to a verbose, tedious dissertation about Simon's artistry, much worse than the normal lecture.

Back at Simon's lair, Samuels had to listen to all the technological wonders he had performed. Even when you followed Simon's rules, there was never a simple "here's your pie, enjoy!" but rather a poetic performance explaining everything that went into making the pie. Samuels never understood it, so he never paid much attention during it.

Samuels made the mistake once early on in their business relationship of being impatient and yelling, "Just give me the damn pie!" It took two days for Samuels to get his pie that time. It took even longer for the headache from Simon's rant to go away. So now he just patiently nodded and waited until Simon was ready to deliver.

The English translation for what Simon explained was that he had five computers simultaneously linked into Gunderson's home computer. Three more were focused on the small network at Gunderson's law office monitoring all data and communication. The office was surprisingly not very secure and Simon didn't find anything useful, but he continued to monitor them for anything unusual.

Of the computers focused on Gunderson's home computer, one ran a ghosting program that recorded any keystrokes Gunderson or his wife made while using the computer. This gave Simon some of Gunderson's passwords. It also took screen captures every five seconds while anyone was logged on.

The second computer continuously ran algorithms to break through the partitions. The third computer continuously scanned code inside Gunderson's computer to find any land mines so Simon could disable them and not be caught or lose any data. The fourth computer was directly linked to the computer's camera and recorded everything while the computer was in use. The last computer was for when Simon was doing the snooping himself.

"I still haven't cracked the partitions. I will, but I need more time," Simon said near the end of his Shakespearean soliloquy. "I did, however, find a hidden file that was not behind a partition. It was heavily protected, but not well enough for the Pieman. It was actually hidden on Mrs. G's login, but she had no idea it was there. It was only accessible by Mr. G. So here is your first pie."

Simon opened up a file with photographs of the Michaels house. The pictures included: shots of Tony passed out on the floor, Tony's vomit, Katherine still alive, TJ still alive, Tony's clothes with no blood in the fire, Tony's half-burnt sweatshirt still unbloodied, every dismemberment of each victim, pools of blood, a syringe full of blood that was used for blood on the ring, the now-bloodied sweatshirt back in the fireplace, the bloody saw blade and finally, the bodies stacked neatly with the firewood. The only thing that was missing was a selfie of the killer holding Katherine's disembodied head.

"Great work, Pieman," Samuels said enthusiastically. "I need all these photos on my tablet, please. And keep working on the other stuff. You're the best!"

"I know," Simon smiled with smug satisfaction. A few keystrokes and the pictures were sent.

Samuels debated rushing to meet Thomas immediately or waiting to appear like he had nothing. If Gunderson knew about his favorite coffee shop, he probably knew about the diner and any of Samuels other regular hangouts. He might even know about Simon, although he was pretty sure he wasn't followed. Samuels decided to be cautious. He needed time to figure out a way to get these photos to the police in a manner that would be legal and thereby admissible as evidence. He couldn't risk finding the smoking gun and not being able to use it.

Samuels met with Thomas a few days later at a small bar in the West End. Samuels had not received any more pies yet but wanted to show Thomas what he had.

After some small talk, Samuels handed Thomas the tablet and asked what he saw.

"Looks like crime scene photos to me," said Thomas after the first few pictures and tried handing the tablet back to Samuels.

"Look closer," Samuels said, pushing the tablet back toward Thomas. "Be a detective and tell me what you *really* see."

Thomas examined every photo carefully this time, and after he made it past the first few pictures, it hit him.

"These *are* crime scene photos," Thomas said. "But not ours. The killer took these as a souvenirs to remember it by. Same as you would take pictures if you went on vacation. The only thing we're missing is a selfie of the killer."

"That's exactly what I said the first time I looked at them," Samuels said with a laugh.

"Where did you get these?" Thomas asked in a hushed tone.

"Gunderson's computer."

"Let me guess, the Pieman?"

"Yep."

"Anything else?"

"Not yet. But I'm sure Simon is busy baking for us. We should have something soon."

"Here's the problem though, my friend," Thomas said, going back into detective mode. "You know the rules, if we got this another way, this would be enough to get a warrant. But as it is, we can't use this. Now that you showed me, I can't do anything about it without getting in trouble. This might get Michaels out of jail, but not like this. He couldn't even use it in an appeal. So tell me how we're going to get this in the right hands in the right way."

"I'm still working on that," Samuels said. "What about the FBI? This man is a serial killer. We have five almost identical murders. Isn't that enough?"

"You know they can't come in here without Ruggles signing off on it," Thomas rebutted. "And there's no way he does that. The chief considered this case closed the day Michaels punched an officer. He wants Michaels to get the needle. He doesn't want anybody looking around. So you have to give him something he can't ignore in a way he can't ignore it."

"All right, let's meet somewhere next week," Samuels said. "Let's both come up with ideas and we'll see if Simon bakes us any more pies."

"One more thing," Samuels added. "If I die before next week, you know it was Gunderson. These pictures will prove motive. It probably won't help Michaels, but at least get him for me."

The next week saw Thomas handling his normal cases and pondering the Michaels/Gunderson situation in his spare time. Samuels mostly hid out in his home with either his shotgun or pistol at his side at all times and tried to come up with a solution, while waiting for another pie from Simon. Tony tried to maintain his sanity by writing in his journal and singing songs. Angelique maintained her warrior mode, constantly bugging Wood and Samuels for any information or any way she could help.

Thomas and Samuels met up the next time at the Dave & Busters inside Stonebriar Mall in Frisco. They figured it would be crowded enough to be safe and loud enough that they could talk without anybody overhearing them.

Thomas noticed that nobody was on the trivia game, so he bought the first round and suggested the two play some trivia with the loser buying the next round.

"You come up with anything yet?" Thomas asked.

"I had a few ideas," Samuels responded. "Not sure if any of them are good. How about I throw them out and whether you like them or not, you play devil's advocate and shoot them down?"

"Fire away."

"I'll start with the weakest," Samuels said. "What if we have Simon hack into Gunderson's e-mail and send the pictures to the media and police and let them run with it?"

"Simon's good," Thomas answered. "But can he do that without getting caught? Media will be all over it, but it might go nowhere. Police will trace the message back to its origin, and if it isn't linked directly to Gunderson, they won't do anything, then claim the photos were fabricated. Plus, once

Gunderson knows, he probably has enough time to move or destroy his computer so even if we get a warrant, it will be useless."

"Okay, what if we have a friendly individual break into Gunderson's and steal the computer in return for something? He could sell it to a cooperative pawnshop, we buy it from said pawnshop and then 'discover' the files we know about and have forensics do what they can to find what Simon hasn't yet?"

"A lot of risk involved. We would be encouraging a B&E, which looks bad for both of us if it goes south. He probably has a security system and our guy gets caught. If he doesn't, we have no guarantee that the friendly individual or the pawnshop owner will go along with the plan. And who is going to buy the laptop from the pawnshop that would turn it in to police and make it credible evidence? On top of that, you know the Pieman is better than anybody the police have. If he hasn't cracked it, they won't.

"By the way, sucker," Thomas added, "I just won. Go get the next round."

Samuels returned with the next round and another suggestion.

"What if Simon gets this evidence to Gunderson's wife? He could write code that would open the file when she logs on, e-mail it to her via Gunderson's account or something."

"I see a few potential problems with that," Thomas answered. "No. 1, what if the wife already knows what Gunderson is doing and is already helping or assisting in some way? Or she doesn't know, but she would never turn on him. Then we have blown our big surprise, Gunderson has plenty of time to hide or destroy the evidence and we're left with nothing but targets on our backs. Based on what you told me, you might get a bullet through your skull from your own gun to look like a suicide. I'm lucky if I get off as easily as turning in my badge.

"No. 2," Thomas continued, "whether she knows or doesn't know, what if the wife is too scared of Gunderson to do anything about it? Maybe she just ignores it, and we're left sitting here with our thumbs up each other's butts, no better off than if we had let this thing go from the beginning. Game over again. Go get the next round. Man, you suck at trivia."

Samuels returned for round three of trivia and round three of the Thomas retort.

"No. 3, what if the wife sees this, calls the cops and Gunderson kills her? Are you willing to risk having her life on your head? Plus, he could catch her in the act and kill her before she gets the info to the police. You know he can hide a body, and you know he won't report her missing. It's just one more dead body that he gets away with, and this one is on us.

"No. 4, now that we've involved Simon, can we be sure that anything he finds will be admissible? Also, can we keep Simon safe?"

"Well, that's where I thought the wife might come in," Samuels said. "If she turns it in, then anything on the hard drive should be admissible. I hadn't thought about Gunderson killing her. If he does, that will be on us for the rest of our lives. That would be a tragedy, and we would have to deal with it, but this is a serial killer responsible for at least twenty people that we know about, probably much more than that. I would hate to sacrifice Mrs. Gunderson, but in the big picture, isn't one innocent victim for the greater good in order to get Gunderson behind bars and keep him from a political seat the best alternative?"

"That's a valid point," acknowledged Thomas. "If at the very least we were sure we could get him for killing her, that would be one thing, but I hate to knowingly risk somebody like that who isn't at least in on the plan and willing to take that risk herself. There's no way we can ensure her safety, and based on everything we know, there's no guarantee when could get him if she disappeared."

"But we can't know if she's willing without laying all the cards on the table for her," Samuels said. "Then we would be risking our case, both in terms of her knowledge and our acquisition of the evidence."

"That's a tough call," Thomas said. "That's three wins in a row, by the way. Maybe you should quit trivia. Maybe buy me the next round upstairs at The Cheesecake Factory. Three in a row. You should buy me some dessert too."

"Sure thing," Samuels agreed.

"Since you asked about protecting Simon," Samuels said with a laugh as they made their way upstairs, "you haven't been to his fortress. He almost never leaves, and nobody can get close without him knowing. He has security monitors in every room in the house, even his bathrooms. Cameras are all over the place, inside and outside. He even has one of those electronic fences that people use for their dogs and reprogrammed it so any time somebody comes within fifty feet of the house, it sounds an alarm on his cellphone. I don't think we have to worry about Simon."

They were at the door of The Cheesecake Factory when Samuels got a text from Simon.

"I hope you have diapers or at least brought a change of clothes because the next pie is going to make you soil your knickers!"

Thomas and Samuels immediately took a U-turn. Instead of heading into The Cheesecake Factory, they headed to the parking lot where Samuels called Simon.

"I can't even begin to explain this in words; you have to see it for yourselves," Simon explained.

The former partners immediately headed to Simon's bunker.

"Spare me all the details about your grandmother's recipe," Samuels said. "Let's just see this pie of yours."

"Okay, first of all," Simon said, "whoever works for this guy does impressive work. I hope you don't find him because then the good guys would try to recruit him and that might mean less work for me. I like the extra money. But this pie is a doozy!

"So I disabled all the land mines, broke through a few of the partitions and had a pretty good handle on the encryption," Simon continued. "I found some files that are definitely interesting. They may have value later on, but won't help with this particular case."

"Tonight, I was working on more encryption when your guy got on the computer," Simon explained, wanting desperately to go into all the technical details of his genius. "Without boring you with my greatness, remember that I have been running a ghosting program and this computer here is linked to his computer's camera. It records everything while the computer is in use.

"So tonight he logged in and accessed a video file, using

a password I hadn't seen him use before, but should help me gain further access," said Simon. "Prepare yourselves because I now have the file and I recorded him as he watched it. I have confirmed with voice-recognition software that the main voice you will hear is the infamous Mr. G. I have also confirmed that the second voice, which you will hear infrequently, is your friend Tony. They must have recently met and Mr. G recorded this.

"If you watch this monitor, you will see Mr. G as he watches," Simon told his guests. "On this monitor is the video file. It starts with just audio. I'd like to know where he got this camera because it is amazing. He must have had it in his pocket in the beginning, and then later placed it in the room.

"If you prefer to grab a laptop and watch this on the commode, feel free," Simon offered. "I don't mind doing dirty work, but you will have to clean up your own bodily functions."

"Just please show us the pie," Thomas asked, trying not to sound demanding.

Simon hit play and the three watched on the first monitor as Gunderson accessed the video file on his computer. The second monitor was dark, but they could hear Gunderson and Michaels talking cordially. Then suddenly, there was picture as Gunderson confessed to a helpless Tony Michaels. They all watched in horror and stunned silence as Gunderson described every detail of the murders and gleefully showed Michaels the pictures which Simon had discovered as the first pie. On the first monitor, they watched as Gunderson reacted like a giddy schoolboy listening to his confession.

"Motherfucker," Thomas muttered.

"That's at Tony's hotel room," Samuels said. "Simon, you are amazing!"

"We said this guy was arrogant, but that is just some straight-up hubris right there," Thomas said. "I bet God is pissed right now."

"So how do we get this out and make it admissible?" Samuels asked, bringing the party to a temporary halt.

"Shit," Thomas said. "That's definitely Gunderson making the confession. That is definitely Gunderson's face smiling and laughing while listening to the confession. This asshole enjoyed killing Mrs. Michaels and the boy, and he must have had an erection telling Mr. Michaels. The only thing that surprises me is that he isn't masturbating while watching this."

"So," interrupted a smiling Simon, "I take it you boys like my pie?"

"Yes, Simon, you did well," said Samuels. "Thank you."

"Partner," Thomas said to Samuels, "you are still the best cop in Dallas. Screw all the protocol. If we get this in the hands of the press, it's enough to get Michaels out of prison. And it will force one of the judges *not* in Gunderson's pocket to issue a warrant."

"If he stores this kind of stuff on his computer, there has to be other evidence around the house and on his computer," Samuels added. "If we put this out there, this video probably won't be admissible, but it's enough for probable cause. That gets us in to find the rest."

"We just have to make sure Gunderson isn't home when this gets out," said Thomas. "We need to be able to buy enough time to get a warrant and get to his house and his computer before he does. We can't let him wiggle his way out of this, even with all his connections."

"Well, if he follows his usual patterns," Samuels said, "the last several Mondays he plays golf. Tees off at eight in the morning, usually at the TPC Four Seasons or at Tour 18 in Flower Mound. Simon, see if you can find his calendar."

"Sure thing," said Simon. A few clicks later, "Gentlemen, he is indeed teeing off at eight tomorrow morning at the TPC Four Seasons."

"Okay," Thomas said. "Samuels, you head to the Four Seasons early tomorrow. As soon as you see Gunderson, you text Simon. If he is there, we have at least a few hours to take him down. Wait until he tees off, and then let's start the show.

"Simon, I then need you to make sure all of this stuff is still on Gunderson's computer," Thomas continued. "If it's gone, you call us both, and we call this all off. If it's there, you need to send it to every newspaper, television station, radio station in the country. Send it all from Gunderson's e-mail. Don't leave anything that can be traced back to you or to us. Make sure it goes to *every* law enforcement agency and every judge in the Metroplex. While you're at it, send it to the FBI, and let's see how many cases they can link to this bastard.

"Look at that," Thomas then said to Samuels. "And you were ready to kill Mrs. Gunderson for the greater good."

"Let's not celebrate anything just yet," Samuels cautioned. "Not until Gunderson is in prison, everything on the computer is admissible and Michaels gets free. When that happens, drinks are on me, anywhere you guys want to drink them. And, Simon, I don't think I need to tell you this, but as soon as the information is sent, make sure you leave no trace that you were ever there."

"Really?" Simon questioned. "Who do you really think you're talking to? People only know the Pieman has visited if I *choose* to leave them pies. I've never even heard of this bloke. Why would I have any reason to be snooping around his computer? I certainly won't leave this bastard a pie, and there will be no crumbs either. You have nothing to worry about on that front."

The next morning Angelique was pushing herself to the limit on the elliptical when all of the television channels switched to breaking news. She couldn't hear the audio, but she slowed down enough to read the closed captioning that was on some of the televisions.

Angelique could see Bill Gunderson sitting with Tony in his hotel room. In the captioning she could read what appeared to be the confessions of the murders of the Michaels family. Angelique nearly fell off the elliptical. When she gathered herself, she called Jake Wood to make sure he was watching. She really wanted to call Tony.

Angelique rushed home and couldn't peel herself away from the television until she saw footage from the news helicopters of Gunderson being pulled off the golf course by the police. Angelique couldn't stop screaming with joy.

Samuels was watching and could only think of Manny Ortiz. He had certainly played his role in this. It was a shame he wasn't still on earth to enjoy this. Samuels had never been much of a religious man, but he was hoping that Ortiz did indeed make his peace with God and was somewhere he could see this unfold.

Jake Wood watched the footage over and over again. He wondered how he could have missed the details. Miss Cook tried to reassure Wood by telling him they had never seen a killer like Gunderson. Hopefully, they never would see another like him. Miss Cook then reminded Wood that the most important thing now was to work on freeing Tony Michaels.

Wood decided Tony Michaels was owed something more than freedom. He decided that even before Michaels was freed, he should file a lawsuit on Tony's behalf. At the very least, Gunderson should be forced to pay for Tony's legal fees, and certainly there was a case to be made for substantial damages. Eventually, there was an out-of-court settlement for an undisclosed amount. Wood refused to take anything from the settlement. Tony Michaels had already paid all of his legal fees. Wood decided Tony deserved to be reimbursed, and he deserved everything awarded in damages.

Chief Ruggles had no choice but to welcome the FBI to take on this case. The Feds seized Gunderson's computer and searched his house. With his computer, journals and file boxes in Gunderson's attic, the FBI eventually found evidence directly linking him to 76 murders. Further investigation suggested there were more but without direct evidence. They could settle for the 76 and would charge Gunderson for every one of the cases. Just for fun, they tacked on several counts for obstruction of justice for the cases Gunderson worked.

Angelique packed a couple of suitcases and got rid of any unnecessary belongings. The rest of her stuff, Jake Wood agreed to hold in his storage unit for her free of charge. She paid off what was left on the lease to her apartment and booked a hotel room in Beaumont.

On the day Tony was released, Ryan Samuels, Simon Gerrard and Detective Frederick Thomas took a $3,300 bottle of Louis XIII Cognac and drank it at the cemetery where Katherine and TJ Michaels were buried. Samuels, who paid for the bottle himself as promised, also raised a glass to Manny Ortiz. The three took a cab to the cemetery and savored the bottle for as long as they could make it last, then took the cab back to Simon's bunker where they celebrated some more. Thomas and Samuels spent the night at Simon's fortress and despite the hangovers, woke up feeling better than they had ever felt before.

When Tony walked out of prison in Beaumont, all he could see was a lone white rental car. Angelique emerged from the rental car holding a present. Tony unwrapped the box and found a travel itinerary. The only items listed were a flight to Zihuatanejo, then a week later a flight to Los Angeles, followed by another flight from LAX to Honolulu. All the flights were one-way and all first class.

"I hear good things about Zihuatanejo, so I thought that would be a great place to start," Angelique said with a huge smile. "Then I thought we should go to New Zealand and Australia soon because it's almost summer there. But that's a really long flight. Most of the flights to Australia stop in Hawaii anyway. I thought we could stay there a while and learn to surf. From there we can decide where to go, but I think everything should be a one-way trip. Let's never look back."

"Sounds good to me," Tony said as Angelique jumped in his arms.

This was not the life he envisioned growing up in the

suburbs of Chicago. With everything that had happened, this had not been a life he would wish on anybody. But Tony Michaels was now finally a free man again, ready to cram everything he could into whatever was left of his life. That, he decided, was the top story tonight . . . and every night going forward.

CPSIA information can be obtained
at www.ICGtesting.com
Printed in the USA
FSOW02n1214010415
6155FS